# THE

# JANE DOE

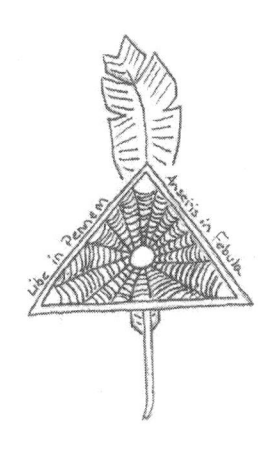

**WILLIAM L. JEFFERS**

Possession of Jane Doe

Published in The United States of America

By Kindle Direct Publishing

ISBN: 9798375967318

Copyright 2023 By William L. Jeffers

All rights reserved. No part of this work of fiction is transferrable, either in whole or in part. Otherwise, it may not be reproduced, stored in a retrieval system, or transmitted in any form or by any means, electronic, mechanical photocopying, recording, or otherwise without the express prior written permission of both the copyright owner and the publisher. The only exception is brief quotations in printed reviews. Scanning, uploading, and distribution of this book via any means whatsoever are illegal and punishable by law.

This is a work of fiction. Except for historical and famous characters, all characters, names, places, and events appearing in this work are a product of the author's imagination or used factiously. Any resemblance to real persons, living or dead, is entirely coincidental.

Copyright ©2023

# Special considerations:

I would like to give gratitude to the supportive family I have been blessed with. I am grateful of the readers I have accumulated and the kind words of encouragement of my community, my woman Billie Jean and Bailey Bug.

Cover Art: <u>Alexandru Zdrobău</u>

## William L. Jeffers

I am a resident of Mason County, West Virginia and a 2004 graduate of Hannan Jr./Sr. High School. I am a member of the Point Pleasant Writer's Guild, we meet every first and third Wednesday of the month at the Mason County Public Library from noon until two in the afternoon. I enjoy life on the small farm I share with my wife, Mam'maw Patti and children.

# When it Began

## 1.

Jennifer Kingston, a young attendant at Cabell Memorial Hospital, exits the break room situated in the east wing of the second floor after preparing for her shift. A short woman in her mid-twenties, Jennifer runs her fingers through her lush curly afro of dirty blonde hair. Her darker complexion stands out from her white scrubs gown and baby blue pants. Her brand new white flats squeak on the white and green tiled floor as the fresh rubber soles make their first purchase on hard material. She smiles warmly as she approaches the nurses' station, placing her stethoscope around her neck. She is greeted by three nurses in all green scrubs, each a senior nurse on the shift and looking to judge Jennifer on her abilities.

"Ready for your first twelve-hour night shift, Miss Kingston?" The eldest of the three nurses inquires as she passes a stack of five thick patient files to Jennifer over the counter of the oval station. Just behind the counter, the younger two senior nurses are rapidly typing on curved keyboards and chuckling behind pursed lips.

"I look forward to the learning experience." Jennifer replies with a warm, ambitious smile. "Has it been a busy evening?" She asks curiously as she checks the clock on the wall to see it is a quarter to seven in the evening. Fifteen minutes early, a good start to a new shift.

"We have only had a few patients come in, but it is early yet." Janice, the senior nurse, reports casually. "We have trauma night this weekend."

"Halloween weekend too." The blonde nurse to the left of Janice remarks sourly. She is a meek woman in her early thirties, not much older than Jennifer herself. They had graduated from the same University only a couple of years apart. Her small frame and lack of tact earned her the nickname Maud Shrewd amongst others in their classes.

"Superstition, Allison." Janice retorts skeptically. "Halloween just brings in more children with belly aches, nothing more." Janice moves over to a dry erase board hanging on the wall with a diagram of room numbers in various colors based on the type of case and severity.

"You have patients waiting," Janice informs Jennifer with her back still turned towards her. "Doctor KLee is on a quick lunch. If you need him, we can page him."

"Okay," Jennifer replies awkwardly as she looks around the floor. She had studied the board and knew very well none of the cases in her arm would require the doctor. Most were, as the nurses had jested, children with soured stomachs. She was qualified to handle that much on her own. Moving off from the nurses' station, she makes her way to the first of five triage rooms.

The first couple hours into her shifts go quietly. She gave out several bandages, and a few prescriptions for acid reflux medicine, and towards her first break of the night she managed to give an overly energetic and fearful five-year-old girl stitches to a laceration wound on her hand after finding a broken bottle in her trick-or-treat bag. Once the girl was sedated, Jennifer swiftly numbs her hand being quick to do a thorough yet quick job of stitching the wound before the girl has a chance to make the task too difficult. The girl's mother, a young single mother in her early twenties, sits on the side of the bed in a waitress uniform holding her daughter still with a panicked expression flooding her face.

"Have there been many of these kinds of cases tonight?" The mother asks nervously.

"This is the first of this nature. Hopefully the only one." Jennifer replies as she flashes an encouraging smile at the scared mother. "It was awfully mean to put broken glass in with her candy. I hope the officers investigating the incident find the one responsible."

"My babysitter was giving them a step-by-step detail of every house they went to and trying to decide which one they were at when the glass was put in." The mother offers with a less than certain tone of skepticism. "She does her best, but she is younger than I am and already making worse mistakes than what I have made in my life."

"Well, this young lady is certainly not one of those mistakes," Jennifer remarks as she senses a tone of dread and failure from the girl's mother. Jennifer kisses the girl's hand after wrapping it in bandages. "It looks to me as though you were given a gift and are doing the very best possible to provide for her. Abandoning your own dreams and aspirations in exchange for supporting those of your child is a great ambition. Better than any imaginable." Jennifer encourages her with a beaming smile.

"Do you have children?" The young mother inquires as she holds her daughter closer to her and shifts her teary-eyed gaze towards Jennifer.

"Me? No, not yet." Jennifer blushes as she sits back in her chair and crosses her left leg over the right. "I am not in a position to as of yet. The chances have all slipped from my grasp. Though, if the opportunity were to arise, I would gladly like to try my hand at being a mother."

"It felt like the world, my world, came to a stop when I became a mother." The woman remarks while a tear rolls down her cheek. The young sedated girl appears to be asleep under her arm.

"It seems to me it didn't end, just took off in another direction." Jennifer offers with a broad smile. "It may no longer be going the direction you had hoped, but you created a new life adding it to your own. That is a great gift to give the world. Your life has not ended, it has only just begun."

"Thank you." The young mother remarks with a more cheerful tone, a renewed display of hope. "It has been a rough few years. I had two jobs until last week when the janitorial company I worked for went bankrupt. Now I am trying to support us with what I make at the local diner."

"Well, if you are interested, you should apply for a position at the new hotel going in on Fifth Avenue. My sister runs it and said they are starting attendants at a few dollars above minimum wage with benefits and almost certain overtime." Jennifer offers enthusiastically. The young woman's eyes open wide at the prospect of better pay with benefits. Her eyes become misty-filled as her lower lip trembles.

"Why do you care about us, why help us?" The young woman asks with a hint of fear that Jennifer may be withholding something. She is quickly gathering her purse, not knowing what to expect from someone offering her aid.

"I just want to help," Jennifer remarks quickly as she rises swiftly to her feet with her hands held up in front of her. "I think people should help one another. If we did, the world would be a better place." She quickly reaches into her scrub pocket and pulls out a business card with a vibrant golden name written in calligraphy across the top. She hands it to the young mother as she scoops her sleeping daughter into her small arms. "I promise, it is a sincere offer. I will have her expecting you." Jennifer offers with the outstretched card. The young woman gazes at it for a couple of minutes before taking it in one of her struggling hands while walking past Jennifer and leaving the triage room.

Jennifer exits the room, following her out to the nurses' station where she leans on the counter watching the mother and daughter. Jennifer passes the patient file over before running a hand through her hair. The board is clear at the moment, the mother and her child being the last of the visitors in the past one-half hour. She is about to excuse herself to the break room when a call comes in announcing an ambulance approaching with a trauma victim. Jennifer rushes to prepare a triage room for trauma while one of the senior nurses rushes to inform the doctor. It is not long before the sounds of the sirens wailing are heard from outside of the bay doors, calling the nurses and staff to meet the paramedics as they enter with a young dark-haired woman secured to a stretcher with blood on her white princess dress and blood running down both legs.

"What do we have?" Jennifer inquires as she jumps in and begins checking the woman's vitals.

"Nineteen-year-old Jane Doe. Blood Alcohol level point eight. Signs of batter and rape, possible mental trauma, and hallucinations. There were no signs of identification on the scene when they found her wandering around the park talking jibberish and cursing children as they ran past." The paramedics ramble off the information as they cart her into triage trauma one. Jennifer immediately begins IV fluids, and sedatives, and relays the woman's vitals to a second nurse. Janice enters the shrouded room with an older Asian-looking man in a white coat and tan trousers.

"Give her two units of haloperidol. Rush a rape kit, and have an orderly get her cleaned up after taking samples for testing." Doctor KLee instructs while checking for responses while shining a small light into her eyes. "There are no pupil responses. Treat Miss Doe for Post-traumatic stress disorder, and administer a small dose of oxygen to get her O2 levels up. I want around-the-clock monitoring and every step double-checked. Do not contaminate any of the samples or evidence." He instructs sternly while looking around at the nurses and orderlies.

Jennifer offers to oversee all the samples being taken as experts are called in from the lab to perform the rape kit. They are not allowed to give the results before the doctor has a chance to look over the tests, but Jennifer can read it in the faces of the women from the lab that the poor young woman had indeed been raped and the fact that they acquired multiple samples, it leads her to believe the woman had been tortured and raped repeatedly by several men. Once they had recovered all of the samples, all of the evidence, she and the orderlies closed the curtains long enough to clean and dress her in clean hospital gowns. Jennifer is not certain why the attendants insist on keeping her hands secured by straps, but as it is an order she has no choice but to comply.

## 2.

Jennifer gives the woman a small dose of a mild sedative to help her rest, adding it to the IV drip hanging on the left side of the bed. As the other orderlies leave the small triage room, Jennifer checks the patient chart, noting the sedative and checking for any contact information or anyone that may be listed to call. She feels a tinge of regret when she sees there is no next of kin listed or any form of identification for the poor girl. Saying a silent prayer, she lays the chart back on the table and draws the curtains closed as she leaves the poor young woman to rest.

Jennifer returns to her station at the nurse's desk just in time to see the hospital priest and several of the nuns from the chapel enter the corridor. Jennifer smiles broadly, always enjoying the company of the nuns during the long shifts. She stands to greet them with a couple of files in her hands. The priest, Father Jacobs, stops at the desk. His thinning white hair is matted to his dome. His long black cloak rests against his ankles a few inches above the floor.

The purple stole he wears falls to knee length with his white collar firmly in place.
"Good evening, Jennifer. How are the patients this evening?" Father Jacobs inquires with a broad smile.
"Most are alright," Jennifer smiles back. "We do have a young woman though, a Jane Doe, who came in brutalized and raped."
"Oh, dear." Father Jacobs remarks with a deep inhale. He uses two fingers to make a cross in the air in front of him before looking up at Jennifer again. "I would like to see her, please." Father Jacobs insists.
"She is in triage, Father," Jennifer informs him as she comes from behind the desk to lead the way. "I was hoping you would come along to see her. I am afraid she is in bad shape."
"The Lord comes to all who needs him, child." Father Jacobs assures her in a stoic voice.
Jennifer pulls the curtain open just enough to allow herself and Father Jacobs to enter the area. Jane's bandaged wounds begin to bleed profusely once again as she goes into a seizure. If not for the bondings, she would likely leap from the bed and fall on the floor with her

17

violent convulsions. Father Jacobs stays back as Jennifer presses the call button for the other orderlies to come to aid. Checking Jane's pulse, she checks the monitor to see all of the poor young woman's vitals are spiking.

"Father, I am going to have to ask you to leave for now," Jennifer announces audibly. Father Jacobs backs into a corner silently as the orderlies enter the room with all manner of instruments and syringes. They administer two injections that ease her seizure. Jennifer sees Father Jacobs from the room so the nurses can clean her wounds and change her gown.

"I am sorry, Father," Jennifer remarks as she escorts him back to the desk where the nuns are waiting for him. "That was very unfortunate. We thought we had her stabilized, the doctor on duty will have to come by and examine her again."

"I will come back around in a one-half hour to sit with her and pray." Father Jacobs assures Jennifer. "I pray she recovers and the culprit is apprehended."

"The police are scanning the streets looking for one or many responsibilities." Jennifer remarks before

18

taking Father Jacobs' hand and kissing the ring appearing as a blue cross on his ring finger. "God bless you, Father."

The lights dim in the wing of the hospital, the shadows fanning out throughout the building. Nurses and other staff members comment on a possible issue with the power. Something between full functioning and an outage that would trigger the backup generators. In the shadows of the floor, the eldest and more feeble of the nuns believes she notices a dark figure towering with its head near the ceiling of the triage room where the girl resides. The shadow dissipates, forming several smaller figures that enter the rooms of other patients.

"My dear," Nurse Agesties remarks with a trembling voice. "May I suggest moving the poor girl to a private, more comfortable room?" She requests as a bead of sweat runs over her pale wrinkled face. Her dulling blue eyes watch the shadows with a fierce intensity.

"We are waiting for one in the ICU to be prepared for her needs," Jennifer replies with a broad smile. "They are removing anything she could hurt herself with while making sure it is accommodating for her treatment. An orderly is due any time now to transport her to a permanent room."

"See she arrives there safely, dear," Sister Agesties insists. "I firmly believe this girl is touched. Whether it be for the good or bad, has yet to be seen."

"I will, Sister, Thank you," Jennifer replies with a large smile. She watches as the priest and nurses move on down the corridor before returning to her work. The floor is silent for the time being while outside of the hospital a storm moves in with the intensity of a hurricane. Thunder clashes, threatening to shatter the windows. The walls vibrate with the booming chaos it emits. Lightning streaks across the skies, illuminating visions of horrible beasts invisible to the naked eyes in the dark clouds. Jennifer approaches the windows to take a look at the storm in all of its wonderment.

Three birds fly into the second-floor window Jennifer stands at, causing her to jump back as they fall to their deaths. Jennifer slowly raises her hands to cover her mouth with the visions of the three Blue Jays that had just flown to their deaths, the splintering of the window spotted with blood from their impact. Lightning streaks across the skies once again to illuminate a large, broad grin appearing in the dark clouds of the storm preceding the heavy rainfall. Jennifer leans towards the window to investigate the face she had just seen when several of the patients in the ward leap from their beds and begin screaming in agony.

An elderly man pulls his IV free from his arm just as Jennifer turns towards the commotion. He rushes at her with his arms flinging out to his sides wildly. Jennifer leaps to the side in an attempt to get out of his reach. Rolling to her back, she watches as the gray-headed elderly man leaps at the cracked window pane. From the impact of his body, the window shatters outward. The elderly man vanishes out of the window, followed by a heavy thud moments later. Jennifer rushes to her feet and approaches the window to see the man on the ground two stories below. His body is limp with his gown around his neck, his naked wrinkled body penetrated numerous times by shards of glass.

Jennifer turns with her back to the wall. Her hands are over her mouth while tears stream down her cheeks. Her knees quiver, becoming weak underneath her. Lowering herself to the floor, she watches as guards, orderlies, nurses, and doctors rush towards the window in shock. Orderlies struggle to get the other patients back to bed making bondings necessary to keep them in their beds. The halls are filled with screaming and moaning. Several patients take to talking to themselves in an odd monologue. Jennifer helps as best as she can to sedate and manage the patients by any means possible. The doctor orders rounds of sedatives for any patient over the legal age. For the few children on the floor, he recommends they be moved to the pediatrics floor for better assistance.

"Doctor Phillips," Jennifer walks up to the middle-aged oriental man. Doctor Phillips has short cropped brown hair and freckles. His horn-rimmed glasses set slightly askew on the bridge of his bulbous nose. He is a shorter man, standing a good head shorter than Jennifer who is an average height woman. "Is the ICU room ready for Jane Doe?" She inquires hopefully.

"Sadly, not." Doctor Phillips replies disdainfully. "There have been numerous trauma patients coming in tonight. Her case has taken the backburner in retrospect. All of the ICU rooms have been filled in the past hour."

"So, she stays here in urgent care until another room is available?" Jennifer asks with a trembling voice.

"Will that be an issue, nurse?" Doctor Phillips asks rhetorically.

"Not at all, Doctor," Jennifer replies in a humbled voice. "I simply wanted to make for certain I understood what was taking place."

"Well, you have the gist of it. Now, return to work. There are patients requiring your attention." The doctor retorts before heading towards the service elevator behind the nurse's station. Jennifer rolls her eyes and begins making her rounds once again. She stops briefly at the bedside of each patient, checking on them and making sure they are comfortable. When she reaches Jane Doe, she steps in to see her eyes open, but hallowed. White has washed over her once green eyes, her head positioned to look at the entrance to her room.

"Hello, dear," Jennifer stammer as she enters the room. She pulls a small flashlight from her pocket and turns it on before sitting on the side of her bed.

"Are we awake now?" Jennifer inquires as she moves the flashlight from side to side in front of her eyes. There is no response, either verbally or by the poor girl's pupils.

"I believe you are in a state of shock, my dear," Jennifer whispers sadly. She pulls Jane Doe's file onto her lap and makes a note of the occurrence along with her current below-stable vitals.

"You will all die before this night ends." Jane Dow whispers in a man's grizzly voice.

"Come again?" Jennifer stammers in a frightened low tone. "Did you say something, darling?" Jennifer inquires as she eases to her feet.

"The son of Hell is coming and he is looking for a feast on this dismal plane," Jane remarks sourly. The temperature in the room steadily becomes hotter. A fragrance of sulfur fills the area. All the while each breath Jennifer exhales produces steam and chill bumps cover her body. "He will feast on your souls, leaving your mortal shells in tethers and scraps for the hell hounds that follow on his heels. You and all you love or hold dear will be destroyed. This sanctuary for disease and famine will be the center of his campaign to end the kind of humanity. This is where he will wage his war, devour his enemies, and cast all of your kind into brimstone and torment."

## 3.

Jennifer stands terrified and awestruck as Jane Doe sits straight up in the bed. The bindings on her torso and arms snap from the pressure of her pulling at them. Jennifer steps back towards the door of the private room, her body trembling, a lump forming in her throat while a great mass drops in her stomach. Her arms and legs feel as gelatine as fear quickly takes over. There is a moment of silence in the ward as all of the patients come to a stop to look in the direction of the private room where Jane Doe is placed.

A clash of thunder and a great streak of lightning close to the hospital echoes through the buildings suddenly. The lights go out throughout the building briefly. When the backup generators kick in, there is a general hum before the lights return. As the power is restored, the lights return to show Jane Doe inches from being face to face with Jennifer. Her dull gray eyes trickle blood down her cheeks, her head cocked sideways at an unnatural angle. The lights flicker several times. With each new pulse of light, Jennifer realizes the other patients are forming a semicircle around the room closing in on her. Each patient is mumbling incoherently under their breath. Their eyes are void, black as coal, and sinister in appearance.

    The lights in the ward continue to flicker as Jennifer calls out for help. The other orderlies on the floor appear to be frozen in time and space while Jennifer spins around trying to find an exit from her cornered position. The patients continue to close in around her, getting closer and closer until Jennifer falls to the floor screaming in terror. Jennifer kicks her way to the nearby wall where she cowers behind an instrument cart and the wall. She picks several packages of bandages and gauze from the table to throw at Jane Doe, hitting her in the chest with both tosses.

    "Leave me alone!" Jennifer calls out terrified. "Someone, please. Someone, help me!" Jennifer calls as the lights flicker once more. The lights linger out for several minutes this time. She can hear feet shuffling and the sounds of several people falling. Jennifer reaches onto the instrument cart once more, finding a scalpel that had been used to stitch Jane Doe and clean her wounds. Holding it close to her, Jennifer shivers as the temperature drops drastically.

The light suddenly returns, illuminating a dark figure standing directly over Jennifer. She lunges out with the scalpel, cutting at the nearest leg to her. There is a cry of pain as Nurse Elizabeth backs away holding a fresh wound.

    Jennifer drops the scalpel, holding her hands to her mouth with wide eyes. Sitting in a state of shock, several of the orderlies rush over to help Elizabeth. Naturally the most popular nurse in the ward, Elizabeth stands just shy of six feet with waist-length red hair, ample bosom, and an undeniable hourglass figure. The orderlies help her to a bed where she sits while nurses see to her wounds. Jennifer stays where she is, afraid to move or speak as she notices a security guard making his way over to her. The security guard, Rodger, is an elderly man with white hair and an unkempt white beard. He towers over six and one-half feet with a large belly and large hands. Despite his size, Jennifer has always seen him as a jolly man. On this occasion, Rodger appears rather upset.

    "Jennifer," Rodger addresses her in his deep, booming voice. "Come now. Let's get you looked at."

"Is Elizabeth okay?" Jennifer inquires with a trembling voice as she forces herself from the corner of the room. "I didn't mean to hurt her."

"We all know that, dear," Rodger assures her as he escorts her to a chair only a few feet from the unconscious Jane Doe. "It was a power outage. Several of the patients got up from their beds and were running around the ward causing mischief. Several of them cornered you while the lights were flickering."

"Jane was up too," Jennifer remarks as she turns to look at the poor woman. "She looked evil. Malevolent."

"Jane Doe?" Rodger inquires curiously. He turns his gaze to the bound, unconscious woman in the bed not far away. "Jennifer, dear. Jane Doe never even flinched. She has not moved an inch since she arrived here."

"I swear, she was up and moving around." Jennifer insists nervously. "She was up and talking. She told me none of us would live past tonight." Jennifer remarks with wide eyes and an expression of dire fright.

"I think the storm has gotten the better of you." Rodger remarks with a slight chuckle. "I think it would be best if you took a break, maybe even went home sick." Rodger looks out into the corridor in a subconscious attempt to keep from being overheard. "I will attest to you being rattled and traumatized."

"I will go take a small break in the nurse's lounge." Jennifer relents. "Maybe an early lunch."

"That is a wise idea." Rodger consents as he helps her to her feet. He escorts her out into the hall where orderlies are escorting patients back to their beds. Two nurses are administering vaccine medicine to Elizabeth from hypodermic needles while another applies stitches to the gash in her leg. Elizabeth looks up to see Jennifer staring at her with concern and smiles broadly.

"I'm sorry I attacked you, Elizabeth." Jennifer stammers with tears running from her eyes.

"It's alright. I was in the wrong place at the wrong time. I heard you screaming and came to check on you in the dark. I do hope you are alright." Elizabeth replies sweetly.

"I will be alright." Jennifer smiles weakly. "I am just going to go to the breakroom and collect myself. If you need me, don't hesitate." Elizabeth nods at her as Jennifer pats Rodger on the hand. She makes her way to the service elevator and presses the call button. She waits a few minutes for the call button to light up, frowning when the console remains dark. She presses the button again and again to no avail. She turns to see Elizabeth limping behind the desk. She begins to sit down but looks quizzically at the monitors.

"Elizabeth, the elevators are down," Jennifer remarks as she looks around the other nurse at the blank, dark computer screens.

"Seems the computers are too." Elizabeth remarks with a tone of curiosity and concern. "I'll call tech maintenance," Elizabeth adds as she reaches for the phone. The lights in the ward dull to a dead orangish-yellow distortion. Elizabeth backs slowly towards the elevator while looking up at the lights. Rodger approaches them with his hand on his taser.

Another streak of lightning courses past the windows of the hospital ward crashing into a transformer on an electric pole. The following thunder vibrates the building as the power once again goes now leaving only the backup generator to power the bare necessities. The patients once again begin climbing

31

from their beds and rushing around the floor attacking orderlies as they try to subdue the patients. Jennifer and Elizabeth begin filling syringes with sedatives and tranquilizers, passing them out to the orderlies while Rodger tries to help confine the patients so that the medicine can be administered.

Jennifer can not help but look at the clear glass pane walls of the room where Jane Doe rests with the curtains drawn closed. She can not help but feel that the mysterious Jane Doe and her arrival at the hospital are causing all of the disturbances this night. As odd and as judgemental as she finds it to be, Jennifer knows in her gut that the poor woman and the terrible things that were done to her are the cause of all of the mischiefs that plague the hospital. Though, she doesn't know why.

# 4.

Jennifer joins Elizabeth and Janice at the nurses' station once all of the patients have been returned to their rooms or beds. Janice picks up the phone from next to one of the dead monitors and holds it to her ear for a moment. Jennifer watches as she taps the hookswitch with an expression of frustration. Not receiving a dial tone, Janice places the phone back on the hook and places both of her hands on her hips while blowing a strand of hair from her face.

"The phones are down as well." Janice comments. "I will use the emergency stairs to go to the next floor for more help."

What do you want us to do in the meantime?" Jennifer asks the senior nurse with a stammer. Her body is trembling. Though the patients are sedated, she still feels the eerie sensation that they are all watching the nurses, waiting for the right time to strike. She turns to look once again towards the room of Jane Doe, feeling her presence at least as a state of mind. Jennifer is still very much shaken from the frightful experience she has endured. Having not been able to collect herself, she performed only minor tasks while trying to help sedate the patients. Her hands are shaking, and her legs and knees are weak. All of her prominent thoughts are to flee and go home for the remainder of the night but she knows the conditions are not in her favor. She will not be able to leave anytime soon.

"Keep an eye on the patients." Janice snarls. "They are still our responsibility. They are still under my, our, care. Even if they are acting as though they need to be on the psychiatric ward."

Jennifer watches as several of the orderlies move towards the stairs talking amongst themselves as they exit the floor. Jennifer looks curiously at Janice who is pulling a handheld radio from a desk drawer, keeping one for herself, and handing a second to Elizabeth who has been declared in charge in Janice's absence. Janice seems to be paying Jennifer no mind as she rambles a list of tasks off to Elizabeth, all of which Jennifer receives as incoherent babble. Shaking her head, Jennifer tries to clear her mind of the numbing fuzziness that has taken over, dulling her mind and blurring her vision. She can feel her heart racing dangerously. It echoes into her ears as a quick procession of rhythmic beats. Her body is cold despite her elevated blood pressure. Chill bumps run the length of her arms, and the hair on the back of her neck curls desperately.

"Where....where are they.....where are the orderlies going?" Jennifer stammers.

"They have to return to the emergency room," Janice replies after a brief pause in which Jennifer's ears pop. "They were only called up here to help in the middle of a crisis."

"We may still need their help." Jennifer remarks in a slightly higher pitched voice than what she has intended. "I mean, the patients are not fully sedated and the storm is only getting worse."

"Calm and collect yourself, Jennifer," Janice commands in a bitter-sweet tone of tainted honey. "You have to do your duty in the face of adversity. I know this is a rather large test on your first day, but if I can not trust or rely on you during times like this, I do not want you in my ward."Janice sneers before heading towards the stairs.

"You can certainly count on me, Janice," Jennifer remarks in a cowering tone. "I will hold my post. I just thought the added help of the orderlies as opposed to three or four female nurses in this situation would potentially be safer." Jennifer reasons with a slight stammer as she tries to resolve her anxious fear.

"In a perfect world, they would be able to help us. As it is, they are needed elsewhere." She stops at the door to the stairwell for a moment to glare down at Jennifer with sincere doubt in her eyes. "I am hoping you manage to stay on at Cabell Memorial, Jennifer, but at the moment it is not looking promising for you."

"I will prove myself, ma'am," Jennifer assures her. "I genuinely want to be here."

"Wanting is not always enough. Deserving and wanting are two separate matters." Janice sneers before walking out of the door into the stairwell. The door slams closed behind her leaving Jennifer to stand alone with her words echoing in her head. Turning on the spot, her eyes instantly fall on the glass triage room where Jane Does stands within a slit in the curtains looking out at Jennifer.

Jane Doe's eyes are gone, leaving only dark hollow sockets. Her mouth is dropped open with the flesh of her cheeks cracked and slit allowing her mouth to open wider in a silent shriek. Her feet are lingering a foot from the floor with her toes pointed downwards. The tethers of the bindings still drape from her wrists, hanging past her hips. Jennifer is about to call for help when Jane Doe is tugged once, then yanked from Jennifer's sight. The curtains ripple from her exit as if a wind were blowing within the room. Feeling compelled to help despite how terrified she is, Jennifer rushes to the room, slinging the door open and entering, not certain what she will find.

Immediately in the room, Jennifer looks around with Jane Doe nowhere in sight. Jennifer approaches the bed carefully to find the chest and arm restraints have been torn free and mostly missing from the bed. The sheets and blanket are askew with a thick patch of drying blood filling the center of the bed. Jennifer turns in place looking along the walls, in the corners, and around the furniture in the room. She crouches down low, not seeing her in the room, and checks under the bed. Seeing nothing in the darkness under the bed, she lowers the sheet back in place as several drops of fluid land on her shoulder. Jennifer turns her head slowly to find two large splatters and two smaller crimson red substances on the left shoulder of her scrub top. inhaling deeply, she cranes her head to look upwards while still crouched to see Jane Doe looking down with her back flat against the ceiling. Her mouth opens wide as she stretches her arms and legs out, dropping quickly and silently on top of Jennifer before she has a chance to scream.

  Jennifer is knocked to the floor face down, the air exhaled from her body from the impact of Jane landing on her. Jane scurries across the floor on her hands and feet with her knees and legs pointed away from her body. Her mouth gaping open as if torn free from her jaw bones. Jennifer tries to call for help, but her screams are muffled in the humid, unnatural atmosphere of the room. Crawling with her elbows and knees, Jennifer wiggles her way to the bed where she reaches up, grabbing ahold of the sheets and blanket to pull herself up.

Climbing to her feet, she turns around to see Jane scurrying towards her on all fours, moving unnaturally and even much so unnaturally quickly. Jennifer screams out in terror just as Jane leaps on her, pinning her to the bed. With Jennifer's mouth still wide open in shock and terror, her wide eyes watch as a black amorphous substance transfers from Jane's mouth into her own.

There is nothing for several minutes. No sound, only darkness. Amidst this bottomless void, a lone set of eyes appear. Seemingly part of a formless face, the fluorescent Burgundy eyes narrow to gaze into her own. Jennifer tries to move, tries to talk, but only an inhuman growl emits in place of her voice. Jennifer struggles to place distance between herself and the ominous eyes. She can sense danger, sense death, sense an unearthly evil that has no place among mortals. Still, the eyes follow her within mere feet. The form of a towering figure emerges from the darkness. A body of red scales, black curving horns atop an oval head of jagged spikes along the jawline. Arms that hang to the knees of unnaturally long scrawny legs. A tail much like a serpent of venomous reptiles. All a crimson red. Genderless. Emotionless. Void of any sense of humanity, any concept of mortality or righteousness.

    Jennifer tries to run, finding her body restrained by an unseen force as she lies in the darkened void. The unGodly figure approaches to stand over her, stepping with one foot on either side to straddle her body. Crouching low so it is within a foot or less of her, he reaches its right hand with long crooked claws over her chest. Jennifer shakes her head from side to side to discourage the creature from harming her only for it to plunge the slender, sharp tendrils into her bosom. With a searing, agonizing pain, Jennifer plummets from the void, disappearing into a chamber of fire where only the screams of a thousand agony-filled souls can be heard drowning out her cries for help.

# 5.

Jennifer closes the curtains back in Jane Doe's room, not remembering why she entered the room but glad she did. She entered the room to find Jane Dow lying on the floor, her binding broken, and her stitches torn open. Calling Elizabeth into the room, she quickly got her back in bed and hooked the instruments back onto her. After noting her disturbingly low vitals, they resecured her to the bed with new restraint straps. After double-checking the restraints, placing the soiled sheets into the wastebasket, and replacing the stitches with staples, they determined Jane had experienced a rather large seizure and that she would require more strict observation henceforth.

Jennifer sniffs the air several times, shaking her head in hopes of shaking a feeling of dread. She comments several times about smelling rotten eggs and copper. Elizabeth assures her there are no such fragrances. She assures Jennifer everything is alright as they finish tending to Jane Doe. With everything in order, Elizabeth leaves the room. Jennifer tidies up a bit before closing the curtains back. Standing in front of the glass-paned walls of the room, she sees her reflection on the clear surface of the glass. Her reflection is distorted, elongating her face. Her eyes are as black as night with red streaks coursing from the corners. Two horns, only a few inches long, jut from the widow peak of her forehead. Her normally slender, lady-like fingers are extended with long talon-like red nails ending in crude points.

  Jennifer's breath is taken from her as she stares at her reflection. Her jaw drops open while her reflection smiles broadly revealing jagged pointed teeth. Stepping back, the curtain closes, waving in an invisible breeze. Jennifer goes to the private bathroom in the room to look into the mirror. Her reflection is as she expects. Normal. At least, normal for her in her panicked state. Jennifer turns the water on the faucet, wetting a washcloth from the shelf and wiping her face with cold water in hopes of calming down. She lingers for several moments with the cold cloth pressed against her face before lowering it. When she opens her eyes, she sees the same distorted reflection she had seen in the glass wall smiling back at her with the tall, devilish figure from the void standing behind her.

Jennifer gasps, stepping backward and slipping on the tiled floor. She grabs at the sink basin as she falls to the floor, trying to catch herself. In her fall, she pulls the sink basin free from the wall causing the water lines to burst. Water begins spraying across the tiled floor, showering Jennifer and forming a pool on the floor. Jennifer cries out in fear as the water takes on a crimson color and two long slender red hands come from either side of Jennifer to grab her hands. Jennifer begins kicking and thrashing in the crimson pool, screaming for help as the hands begin to pull her beneath the surface of the flooding bathroom.

She is quickly pulled beneath the calm crimson-like water, her gown and hair stained red as she resurfaces. Streaks of thick red fluid ran along her face and ran from the corners of her lips. She cries out again as her arms reach over the barrier between the bathroom and the hospital room. Using her upper body strength, she climbs from the thick pool of dark crimson blood into Jane Doe's private room. She emerges into the private room, a pool of crimson water forming around her, just as

Elizabeth and Janice enter the room running to the alarm of Jennifer's calls for help.

"What in the name of Hell is going on in here?" Janice barks sternly as she looks from the soaked Jennifer to Jane, then to the flooded bathroom. "Are you trying to wake her with your pathetic screaming or are you wanting to drown her by flooding the room?" Janice inquires sarcastically. "Elizabeth, go call for maintenance." She instructs viciously.

Janice enters the room and wades through the bathroom to the water lines where she turns the shutoff valves to the faucet shutting off the water flow. Jennifer backpedals to the corner of the room on her hands and feet, scooting her soaked bottom along through the water across the tiled floor. She breathes in short, shallow gasps, her eyes wide and filled with terror. Janice turns to look at her with an expression of bewilderment.

"How are you afraid of a young woman, half your size, that has not moved or spoken since she arrived?" Janice asks in a belittling tone.

"There is something else here. Something evil." Jennifer remarks in a cowering voice. "Some sort of demon or being. They are here, somewhere. I have seen them twice now." Jennifer tries to explain as she continues to push herself further and further into the corner.

"Don't be ridiculous." Janice snaps in a loud, demanding tone. "She is a young, traumatized girl. You are letting the storm get to you." The rumble outside of the hospital roars, vibrating the building, and the window panes as if in agreement. "Being naive and foolish is no excuse for slacking on your duties or endangering patients along with other staff members by flooding the building. You have destroyed hospital property, not only endangering Jane Doe but the other nurses and orderlies who now have to relocate her to another part of the ward. I want you to go to the lounge and wait for me there. Do you understand?" Janice bellows as her face steadily transitions from pale to vibrant red. Her eyebrows furrow and deep blue veins rise from her skin, tracing an angry road from her temples and past her neck.

"Yes, ma'am." Jennifer whimpers. "I swear there was...." She begins to object and try once more to explain but Janice cuts her off with a quick snap and growls

45

in her direction. pointing her index finger towards the door, Janice forces Jennifer to climb to her feet and leave the room.

Jennifer climbs to her feet, sloshing past Janice and Elizabeth as she exits the room. Elizabeth gives her a sympathetic and concerned smile though she does not say a word on either behalf. Giving Elizabeth a meaningful glance and nod towards Jane Doe, Jennifer leaves the room without another word. Squeaking and sloshing along the way, Jennifer walks down the tiled hall eventually passing the maintenance worker and two orderlies. They glance at her in bewilderment and curiosity but continue on their way without a word. The entire trip to the lounge is one solid trek in silence.

The sounds of footsteps, the buzzing of the electricity, and the general chatter of the hospital all have gone silent. The lights in the hall, usually vibrant and welcoming, are now dull, still orange. The exit signs have died, extinguished from the storm and giving no refuge from the silent terror of the entity that has come to them this night. Jennifer keeps her arms wrapped around her lower torso, just under her bosom as she sloshes through the hall.

Entering the lounge, she finds an orderly and his wife in a far corner eating dinner together. Choosing to sit in the far opposite corner, She sits with her back to the wall and watches the couple in utter silence. Out of the windows on the adjacent wall, she watches as the lightning continues to streak across the sky. Though she can not hear the thunder, she can feel the vibration in the room as it rumbles. Jennifer lowers her head and begins rubbing her hands on her ears in a circular motion in hopes of popping or removing whatever may be blocking out sound. Tears stream down her cheeks, and her body trembles and convulses out of fear gone awry. She can not seem to get control over it. Then comes the low rumble of deep sinister laughter.

Jennifer's body goes still and the sounds around her return. Wiping her tears, she looks up to see Janice entering the lounge. The laughter only grows more sinister.

"Kill her." A fatherly voice instructs pleasantly.

"There you are," Janice remarks sternly. She looks over at the orderly and his wife with a high-pitched whistle. "Take it to the breakroom and close the door behind you," Janice instructs in a short but firm tone. "We need the room for a one-on-one staff meeting." The orderly nods and helps his wife gather their picnic-style dinner. Janice waits until the room is theirs alone and the doors are closed before approaching Jennifer. She does not bother sitting at first but rather stands facing Jennifer with her arms crossed in front of her.

"Kill her slowly." The fatherly voice suggests in earnest enthusiasm.

"What the hell is wrong with you?" Janice inquires loudly and rudely. "First you act like you are terrified of a traumatized, raped, Acoma-ridden young woman who can't defend herself let alone attack someone. Then you make a scene in the ward terrifying the other patients, not once but multiple times." Janice barks as she leans in to tower over the sitting Jennifer. "To make matters worse, you make the night harder on your coworkers by destroying a sink in Jane Doe's private room so now it is flooded. They had to move the poor girl into another room, placing two other patients out in the hall so she was not in the room. Maintenance is in her room trying to clean up your mess." She snarls and turns her back to Jennifer, giving her the opportunity to rise quietly to her feet. Without turning back to face Jennifer, she continues in a low voice.

"If we were not already understaffed, I would send you home. Now." Janice snarls. "As it is, come the end of your shift, you are fired....." Jennifer rushes her from behind, pickling her up with an arm around her back and another unnaturally strong arm coming behind the knees. Lifting her from her feet, Jennifer rushes towards the window quickly. Janice begins to scream just as Jennifer comes to a halt only a few feet from the nearest window tossing Janice with all of her might. Janice hits the glass pane with her shoulder and head leading the way. The window shatters from the full force of her body making an impact. Shards of glass penetrate several areas of her head, neck, and torso as she passes through into the stormy night. As she disappears from sight, Jennifer cocks her neck allowing it to pop audibly. A moment later, there is a collision below as something, or someone, lands on top of an ambulance below.

# 6.

Jennifer enters the ward with a broad smile in place of her once fretful appearance. Her hips sway joyfully with each step. Her fresh clothes, changed in the locker room after Janice's fall from the second floor lounge, are a size too small but hugs her body well. Elizabeth is talking to the lesser of the three nurses as far as seniority. She and Julie are talking over a file folder pertaining to one of the patients a few feet away. The maintenance crew is still working on Jane Doe's former room. Wet floor signs set in a broad area around the door to the room as water slowly moves across the tiled floor. Jennifer passes by the two women, reaching out tentatively toward Julie.

Julie, standing a few inches short of five-foot, has long red hair pulled up in a bun with flocks of free hair sticking out randomly placed. A slightly rotund woman with wide hips and well blossomed chest. Her pale complexion is contrasted by a wide spread reddened birthmark that starts just below her right ear, runs down her neck, and disappears into her scrub top. Her smile and brown eyes are focused on Elizabeth and the patient folder when Jennifer walks past, plucking a strand of hair free before quickly lowering her hand to fold with the other under her chest.

"Ouch," Julie exclaims loudly as she turns to see Jennifer approaching the nurse's station. "What was that?" She inquires forcefully.

"What was what?" Elizabeth asks curiously as she looks around. Noticing Jennifer opening a patient folder, she turns to look at Julie with a confused expression.

"It felt like someone pulled my hair." Julie explains with a tone of frustration. "Jennifer, did you grab my hair?" She growls angrily. Jennifer turns to her with a sincere expression of surprise.

"No, ma'am," Jennifer assures her with both hands held up in front of her. "I never touched your hair. I promise."

"Where is Janice? I thought she was meeting with you in the lounge?" Elizabeth inquires curiously.

"I thought she told me to wait in the locker room." Jennifer replies with a shrug. " I went there to change and wait on her, but she never showed up." She explains feebly. "I waited a full break period before thinking I should get back to work." Elizabeth and Julie look at one another before turning from Jennifer, paying her little to no attention.

"Tend to Ms. Jenkins in bed twelve," Elizabeth instructs absent-mindedly.

Jennifer smiles and returns to the patient portfolio regarding a young cancer patient. Sandra Jenkins, a fifteen-year-old young woman with breast cancer had come in for a few nights to receive her treatments. Sandra lies in a bed on the far end of the hall before it turns to the left heading into the east wing. Her privacy curtain is drawn closed but the light from the television is flashing, darkening, and illuminating over the top of the curtain. Her chart instructs for the treatment to be administered every four hours with a dose of Dilaudid for pain. Preparing two syringes, she draws one slightly so there is just the faintest bit of air in the syringe and places a considerable dose of Dilaudid. Capping both of the needles, she places them in her scrub pocket and places the folder under her arm.

Sandra turns her head towards the curtain as Jennifer enters. Her forced smile and jovial demeanor stand as a testament to her strength of will. A bandana covers her bald head where long golden locks had once been. Her blue eyes are dulled with pain and medication. Only the light from the television illuminates the room, the light reflecting off of her pale almost translucent complexion. She lies in the bed with the IV in her right arm, the sheet covering her meek frame with only her arms exposed. Prayer blankets and objects from home rest all around her, and a blue letterman jacket with a large golden 'H' on the shoulder rests across her feet. The bold golden number seventy-seven looks towards the ceiling from the back of the jacket.

"How are we tonight, Ms. Jenkins?" Jennifer inquires pleasantly as she enters the room and passes by the patient to the monitor and machines on her right side.

"Stomach is upset but other than that I am alright," Sandra replies in a sweet southern Belle-like voice. "Members of the congregation of Tabner Moore Baptist came by with my mother earlier today." She lifts the corner of the prayer blanket to showcase. "It made a difference for my morale."

"That is great. Were you able to eat any of your dinners?" Jennifer inquires as she lifts the lid to her dinner tray. An uneaten chicken breast, french toast, baked potato, and a dinner roll are set untouched on the plate next to an apple juice cup. "It appears not."

"I ate several packets of crackers," Sandra replies sheepishly. "I couldn't stomach anything more." She admits with a smile.

"Well, I have your next treatment with me along with some pain meds. I added some Zofran to the treatment, so hopefully, it will help your appetite." Jennifer smiles sweetly as she pulls the syringes from her pocket. Resting the folder on the table next to her, she screws the first syringe to the portal of the IV tube and injects the pain medicine. Setting it aside, She watches as Sandra turns her head weakly away from Jennifer. Pulling the syringe back to add even more air, she attaches it to the port and pushes the plunger in, injecting first the contents of air before the treatment follows. Jennifer sits in the vacant visitor chair while watching the air bubble in the lines. She opens the tray, removes the chicken, and begins eating as she watches patiently.

The air bubble disappears into Sandra's veins quickly. Jennifer places the bones of the chicken breast back on

54

the plate just as Sandra sits bolt straight up in bed clutching her chest. The monitors begin beeping frantically as her vitals blow out of proportion. The monitors read that her vitals indicate she is going into cardiac arrest. Jennifer calls out into the hall, asking for a crash cart and other manners of treatment. Elizabeth enters shortly, just in time to watch Sandra fall back onto the bed and her monitor shows a flat line. Julie enters with the crash cart as they prepare Sandra quickly. They spend ten minutes trying to revive her before calling the time of death.

"Mark it down," Elizabeth instructs as she covers Sandra with her white blanket. "Twelve-fifteen am on July first." She relays while checking her watch. "Julie, will you call down to the morgue?"

"Yes, Elizabeth," Julie replies with a pale face. "Should I try and find Janice as well?"

"I will page her," Elizabeth remarks as she leads the way from Sandra's room, closing the curtain fully behind them. She carries Sandra's file in her hand to go over any discrepancies. "Just get the morgue up here quickly.

"Yes, ma'am." Julie rushes off leaving Jennifer alone with Elizabeth.

"Don't blame yourself, Jennifer," Elizabeth assures her sweetly. "We all lose a patient eventually. Sandra was very sick. She had been fighting cancer for a couple of years with no signs of improvement. I will notify the family, you man the station until Janice or I return."

"Thank you, Elizabeth," Jennifer replies in feigned sorrow and anguish. "All I did was give her the treatment that was due, her pain meds, and some Zofran for nausea."

"That is all you could do. That was what was necessary." Elizabeth assures her. "Any number of things could have caused her death. We won't know until they run the autopsy. These things happen." She pats the troubled Jennifer on the shoulder and escorts her to the nurse's station. "Get a drink of water and I will be right back."

Jennifer sits at the nurse's station with her right leg crossed over her left watching Elizabeth as she disappears into the east wing. Tapping her fingers rhythmically on the table, she looks around the ward with a mischievous smile. Her gaze falls on the private room of Jane Doe in the center of the room. Standing from the chair, she makes her way to the maintenance workers and draws their attention.

"A call came in from Urgent Care. There is a bodily fluid issue that takes priority." Jennifer explains firmly. "They need you to tend to it, then you can come back here and finish this. I will make sure no one enters the room." She assures them sweetly. The two overly worked men grumble as the senior maintenance worker stands from his crouched position in the bathroom with the majority of his anal crack revealed. Pulling his pants up, he and the younger man leave the floor using the stairwell.

Jennifer picks up the mop bucket, pouring the plain water out onto the shower floor. Carrying the bucket to the room of Jane Doe, she grabs a scalpel from an instrument cart in the hall before entering the room quietly. Pulling a chair loudly over to her bed, Jennifer sets the mop bucket beside the bed and pulls Jane Doe's arm over the edge so her wrist and hand hang just over the bucket.

"My, my. How far we have come." Jennifer remarks as she slits Jane's wrist along the major vein, splitting it wide open. Blood spurts into the bucket before quickly draining from Jane's wrist into the waiting bucket. Jennifer sighs audibly bored and grabs the remote to flip through channels on the room's television while she waits.

"Janice Roberts, you are needed in the terminal ward on the second floor, west wing." Jennifer looks up at the intercoms as Elizabeth's voice makes its announcement.

Shrugging, she looks down to see the bucket nearly full. Wiping her fingerprints clear from the scalpel, she pockets the instrument and stands from the chair. Picking the bucket up by the handle, she leaves Jane's room and backs out into the hall. Dipping her fingers into the warm crimson fluid she goes from room to room, sprinkling Jane's blood on the faces of each of the patients before forcing the scalpel into the hand of an elderly man in his mid to late sixties. His tuft of patchy white hair is furled in deep curls. His small, meager frame is riddled with bruises and whelps. The bulge in his pants still reek of the last young woman he forced himself on. His vulgar history is laid out in front of Jennifer, given the night's circumstances. His history is also shared with each and every search in the police databases. This history serves Jennifer's purpose perfectly.

With the blood remaining in the bucket, she splatters more on the faces of the patients before pouring a trail from Jane's room to the window of the floor. Jennifer sighs and returns to Jane's room and picks her lifeless corpse from the bed, carrying her to the open window and tossing her out into the bushes below. After placing the mop bucket in the pervert's room, she returns to Jane's room and sets the machines to act normally as if they were still functioning properly on a loop.

# 7.

A female patient closest to the room where Jane Doe had been began crying out in agony. Jennifer walks slowly to her room to find her sitting up in bed trying to wipe the blood of Jane Doe from her eyes. Jennifer crosses the floor to stand just beside her and places a soothing hand on the woman's shoulder. Kelsey Maynard, a lovely mid-thirties blonde with a meager figure had come to the hospital with an infection in her leg. She is currently receiving IV antibiotics along with some pain relief. Kelsey turns to look at Jennifer with wide, fearful eyes.

"What is it?" She inquires with a stammer. Her eyes have gone all red, replacing the whites of her eyes along with the green around her now dilated pupils. Streaks of red course from the corners of her eyes and along her cheeks as something inhuman enters her body.

"Your due medicine, Kelsey," Jennifer whispers sweetly. "A medicine to treat your wickedness. Your adultery lifestyle. Bribing men of position and power with sex in order to advance your career. You keep compromising photos of your bosses in bed with you for money and blackmail. You are riddled with wicked sickness and this is the only treatment."

Kelsey looks at her with widened eyes filled with shock and fear. Running her hands over her eyes again, her freshly manicured fingernails snag on loosening flesh and pull it free from just below her eye. Seeing the skin falling free, she pulls on it gingerly, peeling the flesh away to reveal muscle tissue and spurting blood. Tossing it aside with an expression of repulsion, she turns her gaze back to Jennifer who stands over her smiling.

"Are you the Devil?" Kelsey inquires with a light tone, her voice breaking and trembling in fear.

"No, my dear," Jennifer replies with a chuckle. "Only a modest servant doing his work." Turning, Jennifer walks from the room to hear gargled calls for help from another room on the opposite side of the ward as the sound of someone toppling aside, knocking over the instrument tray and chair comes for Kelsey's room. A red flashing light and the rapid beeping of machines indicate the emergency call button has been pressed.

Jennifer slowly makes her way down the corridor, passing other rooms or curtained-off areas where patients lay. The blood sacrifice of the possessed is already seeping into their bodies, corrupting their souls, and warping their senses of reality. For the nurse or servant, it is a welcoming sight as the omens that bring forth her master are being fulfilled in this ward of depravity. Crossing the tiled hall, Jennifer enters the room of a middle-aged man with only a ring of hair around the dome of his head. His salt and pepper goatee rests on the tripled chin as it bellows out from under his overly large face just as a bullfrog would look. His rotund body overlaps the joints where his limbs would attach, forming a mountainous blob of fat wrapped around an otherwise glutenous man. Orwin Jennings is seen pressing the button on the controller that would sit him up, but it only pushes him further down in the bed. His bulbous figure no longer bends or moves in such ways.

"Mr. Jennings," Jennifer remarks cheerfully with a broad smile as she approaches the bedside. "What seems to be the issue?" She inquires as she watches the short obese man trying to wipe the blood from his eyes. It merely streaks across his puffy cheeks, his blue lips pursed tightly as he expels gas from the strain of trying to move. His visit to Cabell Memorial was originally for diabetic seizures. The circulation to his left leg has failed, leaving bluish-green veins threatening to turn septic or gangrene. The doctors have already discussed the options of removing the large limp, leaving him an amputee.

"Der seems to be a leak in da woof." Jennings remarks as he continues to spread the crimson fluid across his face. "Idis making my body burn." He wails in apparent agony. "Help me, please."

"Mr. Jennings, it is a lack of circulation in your body that is causing your pain," Jennifer advises him sweetly. She moves an instrument table over towards the bed. A stethoscope, tweezers, a bone saw, scalpel, and specimen pan rest clean and sanitized. They were left behind foolishly by a surgeon who had been debating if it was a wise time to amputate or if they should wait.

"The best I can offer is a sedative or muscle relaxer." She suggests in a sweet, cheerful tone.

"Dat won't 'elp." He remarks while wincing his eyes tightly, He reaches feebly for the tray while pulling the two gowns used to cover the front of his body aside. Jennifer stands back with her hands clasped together in front of her lap. He pulls the scalpel from the table and begins cutting along his cheek, severing a large slab of flesh, meat, and fat from the right side of his face. He tosses it to the floor before repeating the same procedure on the left side of his face, adding a second large slab to the floor where a small puddle of blood is already forming from the discarded flesh and the runoff from his fresh self-administered wounds.

    Jennifer begins to back out of the room as he reaches for the saw. She lingers long enough to watch him begin to see chunks from his stomach and floppy male breasts. Smiling sinisterly, she draws the curtain closed and walks away with a slight bounce in her step. She walks back to the nurses' station and dismisses the alarm from Jenning's room. She just sits down in the swivel chair when Elizabeth returns to the ward. Smiling sweetly, She waits for Elizabeth to approach the desk.

    Halfway toward the desk, Elizabeth notices the blood trail on the floor. With wide eyes and a sense of desperation, she rushes to Jane Doe's room to find her gone. She screams immediately when she draws the curtain back, causing Jennifer to feign surprise and fear as she rushes to join her in the empty room. She holds her hands over her mouth when she sees the faint pool of blood where the trail begins. She follows the trail with Elizabeth to each room where they find a wide variety of dismay.

The first room they come to is Kelsey's room. Elizabeth opens the curtain to see her hanging from the ceilings by some of the wirings for the instruments in her room. Red, yellow, and green intertwined hang from the ceiling a few feet before they wrap around her throat. The wires elevate her from the foot of the bed where she had stepped from. The tray table is kicked over with a fresh tray of food poured out over the tiled floor.

Elizabeth backs from the room with wide, tear-filled eyes. Her hands cover her mouth, trembling in shock and grief. She reaches for her radio with a trembling hand to call for security. While still on the radio reporting the suicide, she moves on to the room belonging to Jennings. The ward is filled with her scream as she draws back the curtain to find Jennings mutilated on his blood-stained bed. Large slabs of his flesh, meat, fat, and the larger portion of his torso lie in the center of the floor as a grizzly obscene mound in the flashing, dull yellow lights of the ward corridor. Jennings lies with his mangled face drooping to the side, his torso shredded with portions of fat and meat hanging irregularly with intervals where he had cut slabs free. Bones shot in several areas of his arms and legs where he had cut deep enough to reach them. Blood floods the floor in deep crimson tar.

"Oh my God...." Elizbeth whispers behind her left hand. "What the Hell has happened here?" She turns to see the busted window down the hall. Walking in long strides, she approaches the window and looks out into the darkness. Jane Doe's body lies limp in the bushes fifteen feet below the shattered window.

"Jennifer," Elizabeth whispers as she turns to look at her junior coworker. "Where have you been? What have you been doing while all of this took place?" She inquires furiously.

"I have been busy down the hall with other patients," Jennifer assures her. "I have only just returned to the station when you arrived. I did not notice anything out of place until now."

"I want a bed-to-bed search. Check on everyone while I deal with security." Elizabeth instructs thoroughly. "Press the nurse button for any you find compromised. I will get some orderlies here as well."

"Yes, of course, Elizabeth," Jennifer replies before heading off to the nearest patient. Drawing the curtain, she finds the sleeping figure of a young girl with oxygen hoses running into her nose. IVs and feeding tubes are hooked up along with several monitors and a respirator. For now, all of the monitors read as if the girl is stable. Her long thin blonde hair lies in pigtails. Her gown is overly large for the average twelve-year-old. Her pale, meek figure lingers in the bed as mere flesh over visible bones. A glance at her chart shows she has been in a coma for over a year after a seizure when she was just shy of eleven. Jennifer smiles when she notices the girl's fingers move.

# 8.

Jennifer closes the door to the girl's private room and draws the curtains closed so she is completely alone with the pre-teen girl. The only light in the room is the faint yellow glow overhead the bed along the wall. Just enough to illuminate the girl's upper torso and a small portion of the immediate area. Approaching the girl's side, she carefully removes the feeding tube, taking care as her vitals elevate. Her chest rises and falls with the removal of the feeding tube until it has been pulled free. Her eyes flicker and move rapidly behind her eyelids giving the illusion she is trying to look around. Behind Jennifer, the light casts a tall menacing shadow with long fingers ending in long slender claws. Horns rise from her head, curling back before rounding forward sharply. Red eyes penetrate the shadow, watching down over Jennifer and the sleeping girl.

"Careful now, Gracey," Jennifer whispers with a crooked smile. "We are almost there." She assures the sleeping girl as she finishes removing the tube.

Jennifer lays the tube aside, shutting the machine down before continuing. Leaning over Grace, She uses a scalpel from her pocket and slits her wrist vertically along the artery. With her steaming blood pouring over the young girl's body, Jennifer uses her free hand to open the girl's mouth wide. Heaving, a long tubular mist of black smoke rises from her mouth to enter Grace's mouth and nose. Jennifer's eyes roll to the back of her head as she rests on the hospital bed at Grace's hips. The mist dissipates, entering Gracefully just as the door to the room opens.

    Elizabeth walks around the curtain just in time to see Jennifer fall to the floor, her wrist slit open with blood staining the white blankets of Grace's bed and her gowns. Pressing the emergency help button, Elizabeth rushes to Jennifer's aid. Pressing a compress to her wrist, she begins the procedure for a suicide attempt of this magnitude. Orderlies quickly arrive and help Elizabeth carry Jennifer to a bed. They spend the next hour seeing her wounds, giving her blood by IV along with saline and other medicines to stabilize her. Elizabeth makes sure she is sedated and fastened to the bed in case of future attempts.

Once Jennifer is secured and stabilized, Elizabeth returns to the room of the sleeping Grace Anne to clean her and her room. She walks in to find Grace sitting up in bed looking around at the blood covering her body and bed. She looks up as she hears Elizabeth enter wearing an expression of fear and dismay. Elizabeth rushes to her side pressing the call button once again as Grace Begins to cry and stammer, uncertain as to what is taking place, what is going on, or where she is. Elizabeth administers a small sedative while trying to assure the young woman.

"Everything is okay, Miss Anne." Elizabeth coos. "You are alright. You are in Cabell Memorial on the Critical Monitoring floor. I am Nurse Elizabeth." She explains calmly while helping the girl lay back. Several orderlies enter with confused expressions.

"We will need a fresh bed and bodily fluid kits. Prepare a fresh room for Miss Anne. This room will need to be sanitized from top to bottom." Elizabeth instructs sternly. "Make it top priority while the others continue to check on the other patients." The orderlies take heed of her instructions and quickly move to carry them out. Within a short time Grace is in a new room, freshly washed and clothed in a new gown. Elizabeth assures her that her parents will be called and allowed to visit come morning. While the orderlies set to work cleaning and sanitizing her old room, Elizabeth sits with Grace in her new room in hopes of easing her fear.

"Everything will be alright, dear," Elizabeth assures Grace while holding her hand from a chair alongside the bed. "We will explain everything to you in the morning after you have had some rest."

"I feel like all I have done is rest for a very long time." Grace remarks fearfully. "What day is it?"

"Friday," Elizabeth replied calmly while tilting her head to the side.

"Last I recall, it was Monday. Monday, May the twenty-ninth." Grace recalls faintly. Elizabeth can see her straining to remember the events surrounding her blackout, her last memories before waking in the hospital only a short time ago. "It looks like fall outside." She comments after several minutes. She raises her head to reveal tears and a trickle of blood coming from her nose.

"It is October, Friday the thirteenth. A little more than a year after

you lost consciousness." Elizabeth explains after several minutes of Grace eyeing her curiously. Fear fills her eyes, fear and a sense of being severely lost in time and space. Blank eyes, almost hallowed from the situation she is in and the way she woke to find herself and her bed covered in someone else's blood. Elizabeth can not help but feel a tinge of pain and sorrow for the girl despite her oath to be kind, but impartial. To keep a level head making it possible for her to make the necessary decisions to perform for the better good. She would not normally divulge such information with a minor unless her parents were present and only with their permission. She is not sure why she just gave the information just now besides the look in the girl's eyes and the string tug at her own heart.
"I have been here for over a year?" Grace inquires in a low, high-pitched voice.
"Yes, I am sorry, dear," Elizabeth replies as she leans forward to hold both of Grace's hands in her own. "I can try and get ahold of your parents tonight Or, your cell phone is in your personal belongings along with a charger. I can get them for you and you can call your

parents yourself. I am certain they would love to hear your voice."

"Yes, please." Grace remarks as she wipes a tear from her eyes. Elizabeth exits the room, wiping away her own tears as she makes her way to the nurse's station where personal belongings are locked away in a file cabinet. She is in the process of getting Grace's phone when two of the orderlies rush up to her with anxious expressions.

"What is the matter with the two of you?" Elizabeth inquires rudely.

"The man in room thirteen has a scalpel along with a mop bucket that has had blood in it recently." The youngest of the two elderlies reports in a low voice as he tries to keep the other patients from overhearing. "We have called security, but he is backed into a corner and threatening to stab anyone that comes close to him." He holds up his right forearm where his left hand is holding pressure on a deep slash mark. Elizabeth removes his hand to take a look at the wound before gulping audibly and looking towards room thirteen where the lights suddenly go out entirely.

"See Grace Anne in room five gets this, Chumley." Elizabeth passes the cell phone and charger cord to the older orderly before instructing Jeff, the younger of the two, to go to the emergency room to have his wound taken care of. "I will wait for security until you return, Chumley."

"Yes, mum." The elderly man replies before carrying out her orders. Jeff immediately rushes for the stairs to the back of the ward, disappearing into the stairwell as the door closes. Picking up the handheld radio, she calls for security herself, reporting a code gray to indicate a hostile and armed patient. Security replies immediately that they are on their way.

Elizabeth crosses the ward towards the drawn curtain just inside of the open door to room thirteen. She draws in a deep breath and enters the room, drawing the curtain open.

"Mr. Tolliver," Elizabeth announces herself as she opens the curtain to reveal the elderly man with tufts of curly hair crouching in the back corner. His gown has been ripped off in some struggle, his IV lines torn free to dangle with blood on the floor. He crouches in a snug pair of white brief underwear with his genitals bulging perversely. He snarls angrily as she opens the curtain to the room with the lights from the hall illuminating him. "This is no way to behave in a place of healing."

"You are trying to get me arrested!" Tolliver screams as he takes two swipes at the air with the scalpel in his right hand.

"I think you are doing just fine with that on your own," Elizabeth retorts while walking around the bed but keeping a manageable distance from the disturbed patient.

"She said she was eighteen, I swear." Tolliver barks with an undeniable revelation he is lying. The expression in his eyes tells Elizabeth the poor girl he is talking about never had a chance to talk. Suddenly, the realization of how his eye was clawed and the reason for his visit to the hospital becomes clear.

"I have no doubt." Elizabeth feigns understanding, hoping she is doing so better than his attempt to lie. "Drop the knife, and we can talk about it," Elizabeth assures him as she steps a few paces closer. "The bandage over your eye is coming loose. I need to clean the wound and rebandage it or you may lose sight in that eye." She explains carefully.

"Just stay back!" He barks as he takes two more swipes in the air. Elizabeth steps back three paces, putting some space between him and herself. "You placed the bloody bucket in my room and the knife in my bed. You did this!" Tolliver barks with the rage-filled craze. "You are setting me up!"

"No, it was not me, Mr. Tolliver," Elizabeth assures him with both of her hands in front of her and visible to him. Behind her, three security guards appear at the door holding tasers and cuffs. "These men are here to help us resolve this issue, Mr. Tolliver. If you lower the knife and toss it to me, they will simply confine you to your bed. If you continue to wave the knife around, then they will be forced to use their countermeasures and you will still be confined to your bed but in a lot more trouble." She explains slowly, in a reassuring tone.

The three guards enter the room, fanning out behind Elizabeth with their taser guns aimed and ready. One is on the phone with the police, requesting their presence on the second floor. They have already been called and active on the floor due to the apparent murders and suicides. Now, being requested once again, the general administrator calls for

Elizabeth on her handheld radio. Elizabeth ignores it, for the time being, considering this a vital moment in the current circumstances.

"Mr. Tolliver, please toss the weapon aside and we can talk this over without anyone else getting hurt." Elizabeth requests as she slowly takes two more steps toward him. Tolliver is eyeing the security guards and listening as the police are being called to the floor. He steps gingerly towards Elizabeth with the knife held out. He has the appearance of a cornered chicken with a fox closely approaching.

Elizabeth reaches out for the knife as they near one another. The guards are already preparing their handcuffs to secure the man to his bed. For all involved, the situation is about to be resolved and the threat eliminated. Elizabeth approaches within a few feet of Mr. Tolliver who stands to his fullest, just a foot or so taller than Elizabeth with the knife held out. He is about to hand it over when he swings in a downward arch, leaving a deep slash across her breasts and upper stomach. Elizabeth falls backward to the floor as two of the guards rush for her. The third fires the prongs of his taser gun into Tolliver's chest just as he plunges the knife into his right eye. He drops to his knees with blood and brain matter pouring from the socket. His body trembles with the energy coursing through him. The guard releases the trigger on his gun, allowing smoke to bellow from Tolliver's mouth, nose, and mutilated eye as he falls face first to the floor just beside where Elizabeth sits on the floor injured.

# 9.

Elizabeth looks at the fallen figure of Tolliver. The Scalpel still sticks a few inches from his eye sockets while curdled blood seeps out onto the green tiled floor of the private room. His flesh still twitches from the voltage emitted by the two prongs plunged into the fatty tissue of his chest. He rests on his knees with his body doubled over forward. His body reeks of feces and urine from his body losing control of its bodily functions when the energy from the stun gun was at its max capacity. Two of the guards immediately rush in to secure Tolliver on the off chance he is not incapacitated. The third calls for an orderly to come to aid her as she begins looking for gauze to dress the wound.

With the help of an orderly, Elizabeth is taken to a room where she sits topless while the female orderly administers vaccines against possible diseases directly to her stomach and arm. After thirty-two stitches, Elizabeth is heavily bandaged. Looking at her slashed and bloody bra, she disposes of it in a biohazard bin in the triage room. The orderly, an obese blonde woman in her mid-twenties, brings her a fresh scrub top from the locker room to put on. Police and the administrator of the hospital busy themselves out in the hall, examining each of the rooms and the broken windows where both Jane Doe and Janice found their deaths. Once Elizabeth has dressed again, the administrator and sheriff enter the room to talk with her

    The administrator is a modest yet beautiful woman in her mid-forties. Her dirty blonde hair falls just past her shoulders in her magenta scrub top with a 'V' neck showing a white halter top. The hem of her dark corduroy pleated skirt rests just inches over her magenta flats. Reddish freckles spot the areas just below her blue eyes and the creases of a lifetime of smiles give her a welcoming appearance.

    "Elizabeth," Darla addresses her as she stands from the examination table. "What happened here tonight?" She inquires with a kind, concerned tone.

    "Ma'am, I honestly don't know," Elizabeth replies. The sheriff stands in the corner eyeing her with his sunken eyes. His deep furrow causes him to almost appear as though he has a thick white unibrow as both bushy eyebrows nearly connect. His thick meaty wide nose flares as he draws in a deep, mistrusting breath. He is a man of stature and importance in the area. Standing just over five-foot, he has had to build a reputation in the community to gain the respect he carries in his later years. His wavy white hair is swept to the left of his head, held in place by some manner of sweet fragrant product.

"Everything went to shit so quickly. One catastrophe after another before we could adjust from the previous." Elizabeth explains with an exhale. "It all started when Jane Doe was brought in. Everything went downhill from there."

"I thought Jane Doe was unresponsive when she arrived," Sheriff Dean remarks while breathing on his glasses and wiping them with a handkerchief.

"Yes, she was," Elizabeth confirms with a nod. "She was kept sedated while some of her more serious wounds were treated and managed to recover some."

"Then, please elaborate, how did this all start when she arrived?" Dean inquires skeptically. "How did she start it?"

"I didn't say she started it, I just said the oddness started when she arrived. Almost like it followed her here."

"Please explain, Elizabeth," Darla suggests gently.

"The night was starting well, better than most nights. We were not busy, there was no great issue or trouble. The shift was going well. We were down a nurse, but we were breaking in a new one as well." Elizabeth shrugs as she recalls the beginning of the shift. "Janice comments several times about how green she was and how she fumbled but would make a good nurse."

"You are talking about Jennifer Kingston, am I correct?" Darla inquires curiously. Darla sits in one of the chairs in the room, crossing her left leg over the right and fixing her skirt while watching Elizabeth. She waves to the examination table, subtly instructing her to have a seat as well. Following directions hesitantly, Elizabeth climbs onto the examination table to take her seat. The obese blonde nurse is long gone, leaving only the three of them in the room to have their conversation.

"Yes, ma'am," Elizabeth replies, confirming Darla's insight.

"Was she inept?" Darla inquires absent-mindedly.

"No, she was just fresh. She didn't have a chance to get into her rhythm before she succumbed to her injury." Elizabeth replies quietly. "I don't know how she was hurt. If she did it herself or if someone did it to her. There are a lot of questions surrounding the incident." Elizabeth adds feebly.

"The death of Janice, your head nurse, was the first incident of the night, is that correct?" Dean asks directly.

"Yes, sir," Elizabeth responds as she redirects her focus from Darla to him.

"What was she doing when she died?" Dean asks abruptly and without compassion.

"She was supposed to meet Jennifer for a verbal reprimand. She hoped if she had a stern talk with her, Jennifer might do better." Elizabeth responds with a shrug. She turns her gaze to the floor in remembrance of her head nurse. "But she never got to talk to Jennifer."

"What do you mean?" Darla inquires bewildered.

"Janice went to meet her in the lounge, but Jennifer was in the break area of the locker room. She went to the wrong place and was changing her uniform while waiting for Janice."

Elizabeth explains quickly while fiddling with her hands.

"Miss," Sheriff Dean clears his throat and raises his dimpled chin. "We went over footage from the security camera in the lounge. It shows your friend being thrown from the window," Elizabeth's head snaps as she looks up quickly to meet his gaze.

"Who threw her?" Elizabeth asks with sincere and earnest desire.

"We never saw his face, but he was a large man." Dean remarks while examining her expressions. "Bulky frame, long arms with his hands nearly equal to the knees of his long legs. He must have been seven or eight feet tall. I have never seen anything like it. He must have been dressed in all black, I couldn't tell you the complexion of his skin." Dean shivers for an unknown reason. He looks around curiously as a cold chill runs along his spine. "Can you think of anyone that fits that description? Surely a man that tall would stick out."

"I...." Elizabeth stops, for a brief moment she feels certain she has seen someone fitting that description but had written it off as delirium. The image of a bulky man, being, towering well over her in the corner of her eye comes fleeting back into her mind. A tremble of fear washes through her body as she uncontrollably shudders. She looks up to see that the sheriff noticed her reaction. "I can't think of anyone that fits that description, Sheriff."

"Are you certain, girl?' Dean inquires skeptically.

"I am certain," Elizabeth replies softly as she lowers her gaze back to the floor.

"What brought on the death of Jane Doe?" Dean inquires, still skeptical of Elizabeth. His general behavior indicates he believes she is hiding something from him and he slowly begins to move closer to her along the wall.

"We were off the floor. Jennifer had been left alone on the ward, though it is against regulations. There was much going on and we each had a part to play in trying to get the ward calmed down." Elizabeth begins to explain. Her hands ring together in nervousness as she tries to recall the entire series of events correctly. "We returned to the ward to find a trail of blood on the floor leading to Jane Doe's room. Several of the patients had been splattered with her blood, mostly across the eyes. The window at the end of the ward was shattered. Her body lay in the bushes below." Elizabeth replies with a stammer.

"Where was Jennifer when you returned?" Dean asks pointedly.

"She was returning to the nurse's station from tending to patients," Elizabeth replies as she thinks back to finding Jennifer sitting behind the nurse's station with a broad content smile. "We started a room-by-room check-in of each patient, finding a few who had committed suicide while she was busied with other patients." She adds while wiping tears from her eyes and a trail of snot from her nose on tissues from the table nearby.

"What were the prognostics of the patients that were lost tonight?" Darla inquires impatiently. Elizabeth looks at her with furrowed brows. Where a compassionate, kind woman had once sat, she has been replaced by one of contempt, doubt, and mistrust.

"Jane Doe had been repeatedly and brutally raped and beaten. Her recovery would have been a long difficult one. "Tolliver suffered from a viral infection that was in his bloodstream, we were

86

starting a trio of antibiotics and infusions. Jennings needed a liver transplant. We encouraged him to lose weight so that he would be a more viable recipient, but he only gained at a drastic rate. We figured he had less than a year left to live. Kelsey suffered from a viral disease. We were treating her with a mixture of medicine that had worked on previous cases, one at a time on a trial basis in her case. We had hopeful prospects of curing her illness." Elizabeth explains, going over each of the patients one at a time while recalling their patient folders.

# 10.

"Was anyone else on the floor attacked or harmed in any way?" Dean asks skeptically.

"Not that I am aware of," Elizabeth replies with a shrug. Tears have been flowing down her cheeks steadily for several minutes now. She grabs a tissue from the counter nearby and wipes her eyes clear of tears, streaking her mascara. "The orderlies and I were going from room to room, checking on the remaining patients. I have not heard of any others being hurt. One patient that had been in a comatose state for over a year has woken. There is that good in these hours of darkness."

"What patient is that?" Darla asks curiously. "I would very much like to check on her."

"Grace Ann in room five. I just sent her phone to her so she can call her parents." Elizabeth remarks as she opens her mouth wide to stretch her facial muscles. In the hall outside of the room, the three can hear the orderlies scuffling about, serving their duties to restore order. From down the hall comes a blood-curdling scream that creates an ensuing silence in the hall before the sounds of several hurried feet rushing in the direction of the disturbance.

"What was that?" Darla inquires with a tone of dire fear as she stands from her seat and backs into the corner.

"I want the two of you to stay here," Dean instructs as he opens the door. Looking back at the two women, he exits the room and closes the door behind him. Darla instantly moves to the door, turning the lock and latching the top bolt before retreating into the corner where she cowers behind the cabinet. Elizabeth watches her with contempt.

"What if one of our patients is in danger?" She asks Darla in a broken, frightened voice.

"There is a police officer, guards, and orderlies in the hall. If there is any danger, they will suffice in dealing with it." Darla retorts as she pulls her cell phone from her pocket and dials it hurriedly.

"I have a duty to my patients, despite the number of guards and orderlies in the hall," Elizabeth responds as she climbs to her feet. "I am going to go help them."

"Didn't you hear the officer?" Darla calls after her. "He said to stay put."

Elizabeth inches towards the door, slowly unlocking it. Out of duty, but more out of curiosity and wonderment, she opens the door and steps out silently. She is met with blinking orange lights. The fluorescent bulbs of the hall lights either hang hazardously or lie scattered on the tiled floor. The doors of the room stand open with broad streaks of blood leading from room to room. The corpse of several orderlies lies torn and tethered in the doorways. One guard is torn in half with his upper torso lying in one door facing and his lower half lying on a gurney in the middle of the hall blocking the way forward. Red flashing lights emit an unnatural glow from outside of several doors. Elizabeth pushes the gurney out of the way as she eases along the hall. She is nearly past the gurney, keeping her eyes focused on the hall beyond when her hand slips from the side and brushes the thigh of the severed portion of the body. Her hand becomes immersed in organs and steadily cooling blood. Elizabeth looks down at her hand where it has entered the vile remains. Hiccuping, she barely turns in time to prevent vomiting on the partial remains. Her bile splatters on the floor with a mixture of stomach acids, grape juice, and the remnants of a pulled pork sandwich she had for lunch.

Wiping her mouth clean with her blood-free hand, she removes her hand from the remains and side steps to avoid her expelled vomit. Continuing along the empty ward corridor, she can hear in the darkness the wild chatter and incoherent babble of several individuals. She instantly thinks of the few days she spent in the psychiatric ward earlier in her career during her residency. Inching along in the dark corridor, she works her way to the nurse's station where she searches the drawers blindly in a desperate search for a flashlight she keeps for her journey to her car at the end of the night. From the darkness, she can hear steps closing in on her. Rapidly looking for anything to defend herself with, she finds a stapler on the desk. Flipping the base out, she prepares it in her hands as the footsteps get ever closer. With her free hand, she continues to search for her flashlight.

A hand grabs her right arm firmly as a deep gurgling voice bellows in a deep screech. The faintest glow of deep red eyes peers into her as she tries to step back. Swinging the stapler, she feels it make contact on the person's forehead, the metallic mechanism squeezes against their flesh, inserting the firm metal staple just between the eyes. The being wails in pain as it releases her arm. Elizabeth falls backward feebly coming to rest on the tiled floor in the sitting position, bringing a swivel chair down over her lap. In her frantic attempt to scramble away backward, she finds her purse under the desk. Spilling the contents out onto the floor around her, she searches blindly before finding her cell phone. Taking it in both hands, she turns the flashlight of her phone on and looks around.

 The bewildered expression of emptiness has taken over the orderly at her feet. His face has been torn so a large chunk of flesh dangles at an odd and sickening angle from just below his left eye to his jaw. Blood is still spurting with each beat of his heart, spraying a geyser of warm crimson onto Elizabeth's scrub bottoms. The orderly shoves the swivel chair aside, leaning into her view to show a thin trail of blood running from his forehead where a staple has been embedded. Elizabeth scoots away from him on the floor while calling for help.

The blank, soulless gaze of the orderly's red eyes is unyielding, unflinching. Elizabeth draws her left knee up to her chest and plunges her foot into the jaw of the orderly, catching it at an awkward angle. The Orderly's head twists rapidly, and the sound of his neck and spinal cord snapping tremors through Elizabeth, churning her stomach and causing her to roll to the side as he falls beside her and heaves heavily before vomiting again.

Using her cell phone as a flashlight, Elizabeth climbs to her feet avoiding the area of bile she has expelled once again. Shining her phone around the ward, she can see patients coming from either wing to the verge in the center. Each of the patients, as they enter the light of her phone, has blank expressionless gazes. They almost appear as zombies as she shines her light from left to right then back again. At the end of the hall opposite her, just as the wall ends with a large pane window, a streak of lightning illuminates the corridor showing the withered frame of Grace Anne standing just in front of the window. For a brief moment, a shadow is cast onto the floor in front of her. A lengthy shadow, both long and broad.

Two spiraling horns adorn the head with long arms ending in talons at the knees. As the light of the lightning dies away, the only glow that remains is from Elizabeth's cell phone, and the two narrow red slits coming from the twelve-year-old patient who is steadily growing closer to her.

"You should be in bed." Elizabeth stammers in a feigned sweet tone. "You are not well enough to be about yet."

"Foolish woman," Grace remarks in a deep, treacherous tone. Her voice vibrates in the halls, echoing along the wards, and drawing the attention of Darla who remains hidden in the dark behind the cabinet in the small comfortable room. "You wish to help the wicked, yet have yet to cure your own demons."

"I'm not sure what you mean, Gracey, but you need to get back to your bed." She instructs kindly once more. "Do you need help?"

"Like you helped the parents of the mentally retarded boy when they were at the end of their ropes? When they could not stomach caring for their child any longer and wanted a way out?" Grace accuses in her reverberating voice. She stops approaching fifteen feet away. Her eyes glowing a brilliant red, her smile broad as it rips her cheeks open to expand her toothy smile. "Or is it standard practice to administer ill-advised, illegal medicines to cause a fifteen-year-old to experience a fatal blood clot?"

"How did you...." Elizabeth's jaw quivers as she recalls the patient Grace speaks of. "How did you know about that?" She inquires bewildered.

"Or, how about helping a man kill his wife by overdose while having sex with him in the bathroom of the hospital room?" Grace asks the question echoing along the ward corridors.

"I don't know what you are talking about." Elizabeth contradicts her in a loud, quivering voice. "I don't know where you are getting this information, but you are out of line Grace, and need to return to your room."

Grace opens her arms wide as another streak of lightning flashes outside of the window. Shadows expand unnaturally making her arms appear to have dark wings. A force bellows across the ward emitted from her opening gesture. The patients and Elizabeth are knocked back to the floors. Elizabeth, who had walked around the nurse's station to stand in front of it, falls forcefully against the front of the station, hitting her head on the corner of the desk. She slides to the floor with a hand on the back of her head and her phone in the other. A sinister red glow emanates around Grace as she levitates from the tiled floor a foot or more. She looks down at Elizabeth as the prone patients begin to laugh hysterically.

The corridors are filled with manic chuckles and laughter as Grace opens her jaw in a manner that would rip her lower jaw from her head. With a deep bellowing growl, thunder clashes outside of the hospital causing the walls to vibrate. Elizabeth slides up from the desk to sit up straight, shards of the sheetrock ceiling fall to the tiled floor as the glass panes of the widows shatter. The steel framing of the rooms bends and bows as an unseen pressure come to rest on them. Glass spreads in small and large shards across the floors and patients, leaving deep lacerations and gouges. Blood sprays on the walls in wide patterns, painting the walls with a disturbing, crimson-wet wash that emits steam in the cold halls. Elizabeth looks up at Grace, her eyes filled with fear and the looming death that awaits her.

"Why?" Elizabeth calls out in a trembling voice. "Why do you come here? Why tonight, and why this sweet young girl?" Elizabeth inquires with steadily flowing tears.

"This hospital, this place of healing, is filled with wrongdoing. It incubates murder and hatred. Nurtures pedophiles and rapists. The sinister and wicked alike are treated here without question." Grace replies in a dooming voice that fills the halls with the smell of brimstone. "Righteousness has no place here. That makes it the best place for me to cross the veil into this world. To bring my children from the depths to walk the surface. There will be no interference."

At that moment, Elizabeth notices a movement from the corner of her eye. Jennifer, with her wrist bound in bandages, fragments of her bindings still clinging to her limbs. She rushes from the shadows towards Grace. Elizabeth leaps to her feet to meet Jennifer at the floating figure of Grace. Together they tackle her with either head on opposite sides of her waist. They push her back towards the window where the three of them shatter the window pane. They disappear into the night as another flicker of lightning lights up the sky.

Moments later, the sound of something heavy is heard as it crashes on the top of a large vehicle. Car alarms fill the night air as the lights return to the hospital.

Darla opens her eyes as the lights return. She stands to her feet as Dean enters the room. All has gone silent in the halls. Orderlies and officers are rushing past the open door to secure the ward as Dean catches Darla before she can fall to the floor once more.

# 11.

One-half hour later, across town at Pleasant Ridge Hospital, an ambulance arrives at the emergency room with a survivor Of Cabell Memorial. EMT workers rush a gurney into waiting doctors and nurses, giving vitals while they rush her to triage and private quarters. The meek body of a young, possibly pre-teen girl, with long stringy blonde hair is transported into the private room with multiple lacerations.

"She is the only survivor of the massacre on the second floor of Cabell Memorial." The orderly remarks while shaking his head in disbelief. "She and her attackers fell from a second-floor window onto the cab of a Ford truck. She is listed as a Jane Doe after the files become scattered on the floor."

"Treat her lacerations," An elderly white-haired doctor instructs quickly. "Administer IV solution and antibiotics. Give her a mild sedative and keep around-the-clock supervision until she wakes." He uses his flashlight to check for a response of her pupils while giving instructions to the nurses and orderlies. "Keep her in a private room. Give her two cc's of oxygen to raise her levels.

Monitor her vitals for the next hour. Nurses spend particular care removing the glass from her hair and wounds before stitching her up. Get her in fresh gowns and a fresh bed."

In the busy activities of getting her situated, none of the staff notice the brief but pleased smile on Grace Anne, Jane Doe. A shadow from the overhead lights projects onto the wall behind them of a figure standing over seven feet tall with spiraling horns and red gleaming eyes. His arms hang to his knees as thunder rolls outside of the hospital giving him an unearthly growl.

"Does anyone smell rotten eggs?" The doctor inquires as he looks up at the nurses and orderlies.

# Part II:
# The After Life

### 1.

"Tim, how are the kiddos?" Jamie, a short-cut blonde woman in her mid-thirties, inquires as she removes her overcoat in the breakroom of the mortuary. Her slender frame and attractive curvature make her a scene of comfort during services at Greenville Afterlife. Tim Freeman, a tall, stocky man of color with a crew cut of jet black hair and a neatly trimmed beard smiles fondly at his friend from behind his cup of coffee.

"Sara graduates this Thursday. She has been intolerable over the past week." He chuckles. "Alex just got his driver's license and has his eyes on the Corvette the guy down the street has for sale. He drops hints every ten minutes."

"Can you afford a Corvette?" Jamie asks with a raised eyebrow.

"I have spoken to him and made arrangements," Tim admits as he sets his coffee down. He came to work this evening in an olive green polo and denim jeans since there are no services at the present. Jamie is in her usual white button-down short sleeve shirt with a dark bra and denim jeans. "I am trading my vintage Sportster Harley and five hundred cash this payday. I am sure it will blow his mind."

"I would rather have the motorcycle," Jamie remarks as she sits opposite him with her cup of coffee. "Your kids are spoiled."

"Have you never thought of having kids of your own?" Tim inquires curiously. Jamie leans her head back and rolls her eyes while laughing.

"I have never thought of keeping the same man around long enough to even have a proper relationship. Kids have never even been a thought." She admits with a beaming smile. All of her friends are aware of her promiscuous ways. She is very active in the dating scene and goes through men almost every other week.

"Children are a joy, woman," Tim remarks with a cocked head and large smile. "You don't know what you are missing."

"A couple of years of dirty diapers and high-pitched screaming. Another sixteen of temper tantrums, vomit, and graying hair. I don't know, man. Plus, I will lose my girlish figure and have to deal with the same man for the rest of my life. At no point will my purse get a break as funds fly out of the window." She takes a drink of coffee and shakes her head. "It just doesn't sound like something I am capable of."

The double wooden doors of the white-washed breakroom open allowing Jennifer to enter. A girl in her late teens with long braided black hair and a youthful curvature body. She is wearing a cropped sleeveless top and snug jeans with frayed holes in the upper legs. She has only come to work at the mortuary in the past week as a means of paying for college. Her family is close to the owners of the establishment and managed to get her a cushy job pushing papers in an office down the hall. She walks directly to the soda vending machine with two ones in her hand. Cocking her right hip out to the side, she looks at her options with a smirk. Her ruby red lips pout as her eyes narrow with black and silver eyeshadow. Jamie and Tim hide laughter behind their coffee cups as she stands with her back towards them.

"Did you bring the muffins on the counter?" Jamie asks with a crackling voice in hopes of shifting the conversation. She points to the basket of fresh muffins on the counter, each wrapped individually in plastic wrap. They are set on the granite countertop opposite the sink from the Keurig and display select coffee choices. A microwave is positioned in the corner under the cabinets where supplies are stored. Four tables are positioned in the small room, each with three chairs. A rolling cart about eight feet long rests along the back wall with additional folding chairs stored securely.

"The Misses made them fresh today. She made so many I thought I would bring some in." Tim remarks with a nod. "Blueberry and banana nut bread muffins." He adds with a smirk as he watches Jennifer bend over to get a bottle of diet coke from the vending machine. He can not help but notice the anatomical details her tight jeans offer as she strains forward. Jamie leans back in her chair to watch him until she stands and leaves. She nods at Tim once the doors close and he takes a sip of coffee.

"A bit young and not your wife for you, isn't she?" Jamie remarks with a blank expression.

"Just wondering why a young woman would wear something so revealing," Tim remarks.

"For pervy men to have something to look at," Jamie comments as she stands. She makes her way to the counter where she picks out a blueberry muffin before returning to her seat. "Don't worry, I noticed too."

"Wrong gender for you, isn't she?" Tim remarks with raised eyebrows.

"Nope. I like them both." She replies before biting into the muffin.

Jamie enters the morgue after the break with a smile. She side dances in the entryway with her elbows out and her hips popping from side to side. In the morgue, a piece of jazzy funk music plays from the sound bar she has connected to her iPhone. Three tables are spread out, each with a body waiting for her to tend to. Jamie dances her way to her desk where she pulls a white medical coat over her plain clothes. Pulling a blue apron over her coat, she reaches for a set of rubber gloves.

Jamie turns to the first table and pulls the white sheet down past the chest. A middle thirties woman lies on the slab. Her face and breasts are bruised, and several ribs are poking through in broken jagged sections. A dry trail of blood runs from either corner of her lips, nostrils, and the corners of her eyes. The once blue irises are now gray. Her long sleek black hair is coated in dried blood and clumped to one side. Jamie sighs and turns her music off before turning the light and recorder on over the deceased.

"Jane Doe, approximately twenty-one years of age. The body has suffered severe trauma." Jamie remarks as she fully removes the sheet and begins examining the female body. "I count seven puncture wounds where ribs have broken off and punctured through the flesh. There are four inch stitched lacerations running vertical along either wrist. Her left leg has suffered breaks in four locations including a fully severed knee cap. Pelvic bone appears crushed and sunken in, the jaw is unhinged and broken in several locations." She uses a pen-like flashlight to look into the wide gaping mouth with disbelief. "A foreign object appears to be lodged in Jane Doe's throat." She comments as she reaches for a pair of hemostats on the instrument tray.

Reaching in gingerly, she uses caution as she pries the object loose from the deceased's throat. Pulling it free, she lays it on the instrument tray and turns on an overhead lamp. Rubbing the object clean of a foreign green substance she places in a specimen jar, she finds herself holding an intricately folded piece of thick yellow paper. A wax coating appears to be protecting the paper, coating it in a glossy white finish. Jamie takes several photos of the green substance that lies dormant and murky in the jar and of the wax-sealed parchment. Using a fine-edged scalpel, she unseals the paper and opens it to its full size, just shy of a sheet of notebook paper but void of lines.

Jamie's eyes narrow as she stares at the parchment. Flipping it over she finds the same glyph style writing she finds on the front. She flips it back over and sits on a fold-out chair to look the parchment over. It reminds her of ancient Latin symbols she had studied during her brief stay in medical school. She tries to read it, her full attention on the paper ignoring the corpse of Jane Doe sitting up on the slab a few feet behind her.

Jane Doe sits up silently, her arms and breasts falling slack as she hunches forward. Her matted black hair swings from side to side in one large cluster. Her head turns to look towards Jamie with white empty eyes. One leg comes free from the table, reaching towards the tiled floor with her bluing flesh, void of circulation or blood flow. Jamie grabs a notebook and pen as she begins translating the parchment.

She works in silence for several minutes with her lips moving inaudibly as she writes out words before scratching them out and starting anew on the next line of the parchment. She is so enthralled with her work, she misses the heavy steps of one foot and the gentle sliding of the other on the tiled floor. Jamie sits back and rubs her eyes with exhaustion and frustration as two outstretched hands move towards her throat.

The lights suddenly go out in the morgue, and only a few small red gleams remain along the exits of the room. Jamie jumps and turns around as the power restores to find an orderly standing just a few feet from her looking up at the light. Jamie turns her head to the left to see Jane Doe still lying on the table, the sheet has fallen to the floor and her head now looks to Jamie rather than straight upward as it had. A chill runs along Jamie's spine, causing her to visibly shiver. She rushes to the table and covers her with the sheet once more before turning back to the orderly.

"What brings you down here?" Jamie inquires as she turns the voice recorder off over Jane Doe's remains.

"Paperwork." The young, shabby man replies as he holds up a clipboard in one hand, a half-eaten roast beef sun in the other. He is dressed in a navy blue scrub top and bottom accented by plain white sneakers. His unkempt wavy blonde hair and patchwork beard give many the impression he is a beggar. "The files finally came over from Cabell Memorial for the Jane Does. Yours here is Jennifer Kingston, a nurse fresh from residency and just starting her nursing career. The one in ICU is Grace Ann. She was a coma patient at Cabell Memorial for just over a year. She woke up just today, during the massacre that was taking place." He stops for a moment and takes another look at the clipboard before he continues. "For some reason, your Jane Doe and another in ICU tackled Ann out of a two-story window."

"Well, it was foolish on her part, wasn't it?" Jamie remarks with a quiver as she returns to her desk. She places the parchment in a biohazard ziplock bag and places it in her cross-body backpack. "Are you the one they were sending to help with the autopsies?"

"Uh, yes." He replies wide-eyed. "I'm Bill Peasley, I will be your assistant now."

"Put on an apron and gloves," Jamie instructs while putting on a new pair of gloves. She approaches Jennifer once again and turns the voice recorder back on overhead. She clears her throat and watches as Bill approaches from the other side of the table.

"We are going to start with a standard 'Y' incision," She retorts as she uses the scalpel to make the familiar cuts on the remains of Jennifer. She opens the remains, folding the flesh aside to reveal her ribs and organs. Using a large pair of bolt cutters, she cuts open the ribs, setting them aside and picking out the shards of broken ribs that are puncturing through the sides of the corpse. "The heart appears to be enlarged and darkened with some sort of black ink." She reaches into the chest of the corpse with her scalpel. After several minutes, she pulls the heart free and sets it in a stainless steel tray on a set of scales. "It is nearly a pound and one half heavier than the average." She comments curiously. After notating the measurements of the heart, she sets it aside on another table to be examined again later.

"Her liver appears to have failed long before her death," Jamie remarks with a slight gag and expression of dismay. "There is a black icker seeping from the organ, fusing around everything in close contact." She begins the process of removing the liver with the help of her new assistant Bill. Together, they manage to get the liver free. As Jamie is pulling it free from the body, Bill fumbles with the scalpel, making a large nick in the organ. Thick black icker sprays, hitting both Bill and Jamie in the eyes, nose, and mouth. Jamie drops the liver to the floor in a hast to reach her apron tail to wipe her face clear. Bill turns frantically to the side, stumbling over his own feet, and knocks into the table where Jennifer lies.

The table tops to the side, freeing the opened corpse from the surface. Knocking Jamie to the floor, Jennifer's body lands pinning her to the floor with

Iker still clinging to her face. The largely removed liver skids across the floor, coming to a stop just a few feet from where Jamie lays on the floor trying to blindly remove the corpse and foreign substance.

"Bill, hit the call button!" Jamie calls out as she struggles to remove the substance from her eyes. She manages to clear enough from her eyes to restore foggy vision. With a grunt, she moves Jennifer from the top of her. Stretching out a sheet, she lays Jennifer out on it until she can get help lifting her back to the table. Looking around the room in her foggy vision, she fails to find Bill in the room. A couple of other tables that had been empty have been moved around the room in their struggle. Several are blocking off the cooling chambers in the back of the room. Feeling her way safely to the doors, she presses the help button, turning on a red flashing light and sending a silent alarm upstairs. Knowing she is of little use at the moment, she starts looking for her assistant, feeling her way around the room carefully.

"Damn it, Bill Peasley. Where the Hell are you?" Jamie sneers with sincere concern.

# 2.

In her foggy haze, Jamie stumbles over a fallen instrument table, nearly falling before catching herself on the nearest table. As she stands up straight, the contorted figure of Bill climbs from the floor to stand just behind her silently in the confusion of her near fall. The black icker has filled his eyes so there is no color remaining. Black and purple veins etch along his face and neck in erratic streaks and patterns inhuman in nature. His unkempt hair is matted with sweat and blood, and streaks of crimson run thick from his ears, nose, and the corners of his lips. A thick white foam flows in a light pool from his dark blue lips as it drops to the floor in sizzling, smoking puddles.

"Bill, where are you, man?" Jamie calls out in a frenzy. Her heart is racing in anticipation and worry. She can feel the sweat running from her forehead and along her neck to her bosom in large bullets. She continues to feel her way around the room, bumping into cadaver tables and instrument carts. Her fuzzy tunnel vision limits her field as she looks around frantically for her assistant. She is almost to the cooling chambers in her search when a hand grasps her shoulder firmly from behind. Jamie turns quickly with a gasp of fear, tripping and stumbling as her legs get bound together. She falls to her back on the floor with a dark figure moving from in and out of sight standing over her. Two others join the figure, one from either side to stand and look down at her.

"Jamie?" Tim remarks curiously as he crouches down towards her, coming just within vision though remaining distorted.

"Tim, is that you?" Jamie asks with a quivering voice. "Something has gone wrong. There was a foreign substance in the liver that sprayed over my assistant and it. It has affected my vision and is acting as some sort of hallucinogen."

"Let's get you cleaned up and sterilized. The security guards will search for your assistant." Tim assures her as he places his arms under hers to help her to her feet.

"Bill. Bill Peasley. He is new here." She informs him as she struggles, even with his help, to get to her feet. "He got it worse than I did, I think." She remarks with a quiver firmly in her voice and hesitation in each word. Stiffness seems to be instilled in her jaw and throat. A lump forms in her gut, threatening to surge through her throat, something continues to strain against her gag reflex in the back of her throat.

"We will find him. He can't have gotten far." The huskier of the two guards assures her before they move away from her and Tim to begin their search. Jamie watches them embark from her field of vision.

Tim guides her to a chair across the room, pushing stainless steel beds and instrument carts out of the way. With her securely in a swivel chair, He sits on a stool across from her and begins using a sterilization kit to clean the thick tar-like substance from her eyes and face. He places large samples in containers for observation and information gathering after the situation has been resolved. Using uncomfortable eye drops, he treats her eyes, covering them with gauze and surgical tape while explaining they need to rest while the medications he used tried to counteract the icker and restore her vision. He finishes cleaning her face and shows her to the sanitizing shower where she undresses hesitantly and only after his deceitful assurance that he was not watching.

She showers thoroughly under his scrutinizing eyes, washing every inch of her athletic but relaxed body. Once she is sanitized, she feels around the shower stall of the towel Tim holds out of reach in his hands just long enough to get a full erotic view of her nudity. Once he is satisfied with the mental image he will retain for years to come, he places the towel within reach. Once she finds it, she dries quickly and wraps the towel around her torso, and tucks it in the front to cover herself.

"Tim?" Jamie calls out hesitantly. "I am ready for my clothes." She remarks in a low tone. Tim exits the room silently and replies from outside of the room.

"What is it, Jamie?" He inquires with a peal of hidden laughter.

"I am ready for my clothes." She repeats louder.

"Alright. I am bringing them in, not looking." He lies as he carries a loose hoodie and a pair of baggy sweat into the shower room. He holds her lace panties in his other hand, holding them up to his nose as he takes a deep whiff.

"Do you need help?" Tim offers in mock kindness.

"I can manage, but thank you. You are very kind." Jamie remarks sweetly with a hesitant smile.

"It is not like you have anything I haven't seen a thousand times before," Tim assures her as he places the clothes, along with the crumpled lace panties, into her hands.

"It wasn't mine those times, and I want it to remain that way, Tim. Our working relationship depends on it." Jamie remarks sternly while maintaining the forced yet teasing smile.

"Well, I will be right outside if you need anything," Tim replies with a light laugh.

"Close the door on your way out, please." Jamie requests with a smile and chuckle.

Tim walks over to the door, making a point for his footsteps to be heard. He stands just within the room as he pushes the door closed and silently steps to the side where three chairs are lined up along the wall opposite the shower stall. He gently sits down with his attention fully on her as she waits a few moments with her head cocked to one side. With mild certainty and wistful hopes of sincerity and genuine chivalry on Tim's part, she pulls the towel from her body with her clothes still in her hand. Placing her panties and sweats between her thighs, she raises her arms over her head and pulls the Crimson High hoodie on over her still damp torso. Pulling her wet, matted hair from within the hoodie, she lets it trail over her left shoulder. Holding her sweats under her arm and leaning against a wall adjacent to the shower, she pulls her panties on one leg at a time before pulling them up over her tush to her just above her hips. Using the wall for balance, she pulls her sweats on similarly before pulling them up just above her lacy panties.

With her dressed and beginning to move towards the door, Tim stands and crosses five feet to the door and opens it silently. Stepping out, he pulls the door to before releasing the nob and allowing it to click into place silently. With a large smile and bulging trousers, he rests with his back against the wall to the left of the door. The door opens outwards to reveal the currently blinded Jamie with her dark matted wet hair, her right arm outstretched with open fingers, grasping at air. Tim steps out away from the wall and takes her by the hand.

"I'm right here, Jamie." He remarks with kind assurance. "Feeling alright?" He asks sincerely as he takes her by the arm and guides her to a secure room where an orderly is preparing a bed in a softly lit room. He guides her to the bed as she formulates an answer.

"My stomach is knotted up." She admits sheepishly. She looks in the direction of her arm as the female orderly raises her hoodie sleeve to place an IV line.

"You will feel a tiny prick, Jamie." She whispers softly. The orderly, a young woman in her early twenties with long auburn hair and a very modest petite body, wipes the bend of Jamie's elbow with an alcohol wipe and gauze before inserting the IV needle with a less than delicate touch. Jamie flinches and lets out a hiss as the orderly places the surgical tape over the butterfly needle to hold it securely in place. As she is hooking up the IV lines and securing the saline solution, Jamie looks in her direction.

"Hannah, right?" Jamie comments casually with a sense of the space around her.

"Yeah, a first-year resident. I just finished training at the career center." Hannah replies with a smile. "I was ordered to set you up on IV saline fluids, IV antibiotics, and to administer a light sedative to help you relax while your eyes heal." She informs Jame while leaning on the handrails of the bed as if having a conversation with the currently blinded patient. With Hannah's attention diverted and Jamie incapable of seeing what he is doing, Tim steps to the side where the medications are resting in a blue caddy on a stainless steel instrument table. The various syringes are marked by color code and name and prepared for the individual rooms where they are to be given to patients. He located the sedative that is intended for Jamie and swaps the syringe out for one he has waiting in his pocket. With the switch made, and their conversation coming to an end, he steps away with his hands in his pockets and a broad smile on his face.

"Is she going to be able to rest comfortably, Hannah?" Tim inquires as she turns back to her caddy and reaches for the sedative. Screwing the syringe into the administering port, she injects the medicine slowly.

"She will be comfortable, but aware," Hannah replies with a smile. She removes the sedative and replaces it with a saline syringe to flush the port. "I am going to turn the lights down a little bit more as I leave, but she should be able to rest comfortably."

"Well, I have to return to the Emergency Room," Tim remarks audibly. "But I will come by and check on you later when I take a break."

"Alright." Jamie retorts as she lays back on the hospital bed. "A corpse is lying on the floor in the morgue. She fell on me when the table tipped over in excitement." She informs him as the thought occurs to her. "When they find Bill, he is likely worse than I am. He will need medical assistance. I also have two other bodies in the morgue that need to be placed in the coolers." She rambles off details as the sedative begins to take effect. She finds herself relaxing and finding a place where she can rest. She hears Tim make some reply, not really concerned with what he is saying, before walking from the room. It is a matter of moments before she hears Hannah follow him, closing the door to the room behind her. The last conscious thought she recalls having is an image of a tall dark figure with red gleaming eyes. His arms hang to his knees, ending in sharp claws. Spiraling claws coil on either side of his head where long pointed ears rest comfortably.

"You have been deceived, child." An ominous and sinister voice remarks with an acidic giggle of glee. " You have been drugged to find no consciousness. In a matter of hours, your body will be defiled by the very friend you claim to know. Your assistant, my devout follower, moves to claim souls for my rebirth, the lost child spreads my body as a plague. You will all die tonight."

# 3.

After the black icker exploded into his face, Bill stumbled backward, tripping over his own feet. His head finds purchase on the nearby slab where the corpse of a rather obese man lies, a container of his severed body meat rests at his feet. In the fall, and with the force of the impact of his head on the table, his neck snaps viciously to the side causing instant death. With his body lying motionless on the floor, the black icker bubbles over his eyes as the whites absorb the vile substance, sucking it in. Icker oozes into his open mouth, a lump forming in the top of his throat and visibly working its way down his awkwardly twisted neck. Blood runs from his ears, dripping to the floor to form a quarter-sized puddle.

Jamie wanders around and stumbles past him to hit the alarm button by the door. His hopeless, dead, and expressionless face watches her in unknown torment as his soul tries to move on but is held at bay by the unearthly entity spreading through his body by means of the thick icker. Rolling to his side, his mouth opens wide in a silent scream of agony. His arms contort in an unnatural claw-like position with his palms flat on the floor. His legs swivel to either side as if on hinged, and his ankles break as his feet turn to face forward making him into a bipedal creature of darkness. With his complexion turning paler by the second, his lips going from a rosy red to an icy blue, he scurries from the room on all four into the hall and disappears in the shadows of the basement corridor.

Crawling along the wall to the ceiling of the corridor, he watches as the elevator opens. Four individuals rush from the open compartment towards the morgue. Two guards, a nurse, and a doctor. With their attention focused on the morgue, Bill scurries rapidly across the roof to the closing doors of the lift. Narrowly getting through before they close, the doors seal behind him as he releases his hands from the roof of the lift allowing him to stand tall from the ceiling and press the six button repeatedly. The lift begins moving, rising floor by floor on its way towards the cancer ward of the hospital.

The lift stops unexpectedly on the third floor. A new mother, a young woman maybe in her mid to late teens with bushy red hair, sits in a wheelchair handled by a midwife. The young woman's cynical yet haughty mother stands next to her. The older woman has a salt and pepper bob cut and remains of fresh cat hair rest on the shoulders of her light blue day coat. She carries a large handbag in her left hand with the right tremors holding an unlit cigarette to her lips.

"Ma'am, the hospital is a no tobacco zone." The midwife reminds her sternly. In her late thirties, the midwife has a slightly robust waistline with large breasts and hips, with a rather nonproportional small upper torso and thin legs. Her fluffy, curly blonde hair is reminiscent of the sixties big hairstyle with a pink rose stuck behind her right ear.

"Well, it's not lit now is it?" The older woman retorts sarcastically. She drags on the filter of the unlit cigarette again while looking the midwife directly in the eyes.

"Mom, can you just put it away until we are in the car?" The young mother inquires with a frail, embarrassed voice. The doors finally close, sealing shut. The lift jars as it begins rising again. The midwife looks at the digital screen highlighting the floor numbers as a trail of black icker runs from the ceiling of the lift to trail softly into her hair and down her back.

"If you had kept your legs closed, we wouldn't be here in the first place, Amanda." Her mother remarks sourly. "Now, instead of getting to enjoy my golden years, I have to help you raise that mistake of a child you hold in your arms."

"Mom," Amanda cuts into the thick despise coming from her mother's voice. "She may not have been planned, and I may have been doing wrong to conceive her, but she is no mistake and I love her. Her name is Auror and you will love her too."

"Auror," The woman huffs. "Not only do you make yourself into a whore, but you defile our family by naming the runt after a fantasy character from one of your books."

"Ma'am," The midwife snaps. "If you do not change your attitude, I will be forced to call in Child Protective Services." She threatens tensely.

"Will they take the little bitch away?" The woman turns to her with a hopeful expression. At her words, the girl begins crying.

The Midwife holds a finger up, pointing towards the ceiling, and purses her lips in preparation to rip the sour woman verbally when both women see a trail of black icker stream from the ceiling to the floor. The lift doors open as both women slowly raise their gaze to follow the thick, clingy trail. Their eyes grow wide and their jaws drop in silent horror. The midwife shoves the wheelchair with the young mother and her child from the lift onto the sixth floor just before the doors close. The foul woman tries to make a run for the door as the opening is reduced to a narrow slit, but a long clawed hand reaches around her throat and drags her back. The door closes, and the clicking as it seals closes off the screams of horror that fill the small space.

On the fourth floor, the lift dings as it comes to a stop. Three individuals stand outside of the two-sided door. One, a mother of five with straight brown hair and a still jovial smile, stands carrying a baby in one arm and her backpack slung over the other. She can be no older than twenty-five, though the experience in her brown eyes speaks volumes. In the second, a doctor of podiatry stands in a white gown running his fingers through his wavy black hair. The third is an elderly British soldier on holiday. His wrinkly bald head shows several liver spots. His white mustache nestles just over his lower lip, thick in volume and luscious. He is wearing his best blue suit over a white button-down shirt, black leather belt, and blue trousers over black loafers. His wooden shepherd's hook cane shivers under his tremorous right hand, excess skin folding over the arch of the cane as he leans on the wooden appendage.

The door to the lift opens, leaving a moment of silence to echo in the white-washed tiled corridor of the fourth floor before the inhabitants of the waiting room behind the unfortunate three individuals begin screaming in horror. Several of the women sitting closest to the lift begin vomiting violently at their feet. The British soldier steps back with wide eyes. The podiatrist falls to his knees in prayer. The young mother of five turns to shield her baby as she takes off running down the hall, pale as a ghost and crying. The horror within the lift becomes visible as unnatural darkness fades, allowing light to enter once more.

Red shimmering high heels lay haphazardly with the feet they shielded still resting within. The feet are severed at the ankles with a ruby ankle bracelet barely clinging to flesh. The walls that were once white are now congealing crimson with chunks of pale tan flesh sticking as a crude decoration. Strings of the intestine and bodily veins stick to the walls in a grizzly scene. There are no full remains aside from the feet in the high heels. There is an absence of distinguishable organs or appendages. Blood drips as rain from the ceiling where a crimson-coated bipedal creature with black orbs for eyes moves slowly, unseen as it blends in with the gore of the chamber.

The British soldier grasps his left breast as his eyes grow wide. His mouth contorts in an oval cry of pain as he drops first to one knee before caving to his side. He tears at his shirt, ripping it open as he closes his eyes tightly. His struggle lasts only a few minutes before he goes limp.

At the nurse's station, an elderly white-haired nurse is on the phone, calling in the disturbance to security. The other three nurses in the area rush around trying to tend to the patients in the waiting room. They try to triage immediate reactions to the scene of the lift. Several of the elderly patients are falling to the floor in either a stroke or heart complications. The younger adults are either too busy vomiting or having panic attacks that cause more issues for the nursing staff. Mothers are shielding their children and their eyes from the scene. Children are crying and cowering in the corners of the room, behind furniture, and their parents. One preteen-blonde girl who had been playing in the center of the carpeted waiting area begins rushing toward her mother. One rather eccentric man who had fallen to the floor begins to panic as his full vision takes in the scene of the lift. He leaps to his feet and turns to run. As he turns, he plows into the girl, trampling her to the ground. The heel of his suede loafer crushes her weak throat and snaps her neck. The girl's mother watches in horror as her daughter is killed by the foot of the man in a rug suit.

"You cowardly bastard!" She cries out loud as she climbs through her own vomit to her feet. Rushing across the floor towards him. She wraps her arms around the man as she catches up to him, forcing the energy of her tackle to commute through him. The pair fall towards the window nearby, crashing through and falling from sight. The storm outside becomes known as thunder clashes through the now open window.

With the initial opening of the lift causing utter chaos, devastating the peace of the foyer on the fourth floor, The crimson bipedal figure crawls from the open lift doors onto the ceiling of the fourth floor. The fourth floor is intended for general doctorings, podiatry, pediatrics, and radiology. Broken into four parts with the lift in the center of the floor, the bipedal creature crawls around to the northern side of the lift divider where it comes to a stop just behind the desk of a receptionist. The lights of the floor fade in and out before the fluorescent bulbs die entirely. Blanketed in darkness the patients, nurses, and receptionists of the fourth floor were in a full-on panic. They begin running towards the emergency exit to enter the stairwell. As they get close, they see a dark figure rise from the floor. Spiraling horns adorn either side of its heart. Red narrowed eyes look down at them as their arms hang menacingly to knee length curling into claws.

# 4.

The darkness spreads from the center of the fourth floor and each of the corners, taking over the floor until the darkness left from the lights going out has deepened to an unnatural thickness. The looming figure of dreadful black is outlined with an insidious shadow making it barely visible in the blackout. Thunder clashes again as a streak of lightning arcs across the sky in the distance. The city is highlighted as the yellowish bolt casts a dim light for a brief moment. Towering structures of ominous depths stand over scattered yet structured buildings that form a spider web of streets, all leading towards the hospital. Bill scurries along the ceiling while the patients and their children try to find somewhere to hide from the menacing shadow.

    Patients are heading down the hall, finding offices to hide in, all trying to find another exit from the fourth floor since the elevator is covered in gore and death, the emergency exit cut off by the dark entity. Thunder vibrates the building once again as the storm threatens to bring it crashing down.

Jamie has slipped into a deep sleep, her dreams filled with a parking garage that spirals downwards. The floor is a bubbling red icker of lava and flames, and the painted lands of the parking spaces appear as dried crimson blood. Instead of vehicles in the parking spaces, hospital gurneys rest in place with a tripod holding IV fluids. The handrails are adorned with restraint straps for wrists and ankles. Jamie walks softly, her feet finding each step taking another layer of flesh from her feet. As hot as the garage is, the humidity causes layers of skin to melt and drip onto the surface causing a spout of steam to rise as it hisses. She looks around the garage as wails of anguish and pain come from every corner and every curve.

    She watches as goblin-sized creatures with curved horns and bile-green flesh scurry from behind her. They rush towards her with empty hollow eye sockets. Jamie tries to begin to run in her hospital gown, her feet melting deeper and deeper into the soft molten ground. She turns back to look, counting six of the menacing creatures making chase. As her feet continue to sink until they are reduced to nubs at her shin with only exposed bone remaining below the smoking, molting flesh below her knee, the imps catch up to her. They lift her from the molten floor to their shoulders. The wails grow louder, more horrific as the imps carry her to a gurney in parking slot sixty-nine. They fling her to the cot, strapping down her arms and placing the straps around the bones of her ankles. A wide strap is flung across her waist and anchored down while an imp with a surgical mask inserts a butterfly needle in her right elbow.

They speak in some dark speech that resembles gurgling and hissing. Jamie looks from side to side, calling for help. She yells for several minutes before she realizes her cries for help have joined the wails that fill the parking garage. She struggles in dismay as the imp with the surgical mask climbs on top of the bed and straddles her with a scalpel. He slits her hospital gown down the center, stripping her bare on the gurney while laughing psychotically.

He runs the scalpel along the inside of her forearm, leaving deep lacerations before using it to branch off of the original lacerations to form trees of blood on her forearms. Using hemostats to pull her veins from her arms, tethering them together in the center and anchoring them to the bed above her head. He continues to laugh as he removes her upper and lower eyelids. They strap her head in place so her view is fixated on the roof of the parking garage level. From wall to wall it is a ceiling of swirling arrays of orange and red flames licking and lashing out in every direction. She can see nothing but the flames. No hope, no chance of redemption or freedom. Only endless flames.

She can feel the imps scurry from her side. There is a moment when the only sound is that of the persistent wailing that fills the garage. There is no comfort to be found in the garage. She tries to squirm, trying to find an inch of movement or any advantage to regain her freedom. The heat of the garage, the insidious, ominous flaming garage continues to melt her flesh, removing layers and layers until she is left in a seeping puddle of her own liquified flesh. Her body is reduced to muscle tissue and fatty gristle with the exception of her legs which are nothing but bone from the shin down.

"Ah, there you are, Jamie." The embodied voice of Tim comes as a pleasant surprise as her tear-filled eyes search the room rapidly.

"Tim, where are you?" Jamie calls out frantically. "Let me free, please." She pleads as she pulls once more at her bindings. She can feel the pressure of weight on the gurney between her wide-bound legs and around her torso. She tries to peer down past her bosom but can only see the dark icker walls that form the center of the parking garage.

There is a moment of pressure in her pelvic area before she cries out in agony. Her lower torso begins to contort before a fire-like penetration runs from her inner thighs into her pelvic area before entering her lower stomach. She cries out in pain as her lower torso feels as though it is being ripped apart. She can feel a pressure that begins in either inner thigh forming a tear straight up the center of her pelvic and stomach. Her breasts are pressed in and to either side while an acid is invisibly run across her throat, down between her breasts. She is tasseled up and down, from side to side while restrained on the gurney. She tries to close her eyes against the pain but only forms thicker, more substantial tears in place of her eyelids.

A heavy pressure makes its way up her torso as the pain and devastation in her inner thighs and pelvic continues to grow. She peers all around her, struggling against the restraint that is holding her head in place. Her pupils grow as the dark figure looms into view. His curling horns have streaks of brown and black. His flesh is red and porous. He looks at her with red menacing eyes and slits in place of a natural nose. His broad shoulders linger a human length on either side of the bed with his sternum resting just above her. He releases his long forked tongue to lick her throat and chin, his saliva burns like liquid fire.

"Why?" She tries to gurgle. Blood spurts from her mouth, covering her chin, and neck, and blurs her vision as it covers her eyes. The pain intensifies below her navel, the sensation is unlike any pain she has ever felt or imagined as her legs are forced further apart despite her struggle.

"You are to be my instrument, you and the lost one." The entity growls as he rakes his claws down her chest, tearing away muscle tissue and tendons. His breath smells of brimstone, rotten eggs, and of decomposing corpses. Aside from the blood still seeping from the corners of her mouth, bile rises and spills over the sides as she begins to drown in her own vomit. Heaving with her chest struggling to rise and fall with the lack of incoming air, she spews vomit down either cheek. He leans in, his nostril slits widening as he takes in her dying scent.

"You are weak, fragile." He grumbles in a rocky, sulfuric air. "You are a pawn in the meaningless struggle of humanity. Why even fight my influence?" He snarls. His jagged, misshapen teeth grind close inches from her chin.

Unable to reply, tears and blood run from the corners of her eyes as she tries to move her head away from him. If his reaction could be called a smile, the seams of his mouth cut into what would be cheekbones. His lipless mouth exposed his grizzly teeth even more than before. Blackness flashes in front of her eyes. The figure disappears from her sight.

Jamie feels the restraints disappear, freeing her in the fiery inferno of a hospital room within the garage. The looming figure is replaced by the image of Tim who crouches over her, between her thighs with his pants down. An immense rage and unnatural hatred, even at the moment, fill her. An entity beyond her understanding empowers her strength while draining her humanity. She reaches up rapidly, without thought or warning. She cups either side of his head in her hands and the same motion twists it violently, turning his head so his gaze is looking behind himself. Pushing Tim aside, she looks down at her fleshless, nude body. Reaching above her head, she blindly fumbles with a knot of veins within her vision.

In the ICU, the room marked Jane Doe is filled with nurses and orderlies tending to the wounded patient brought in from Cabell Memorial. The young girl who they now know to be Grace Ann had been a coma patient. The hospital floor had been in chaos when she woke. In a matter of an hour, she was tackled from the second-floor window to the top of a vehicle below. The doctor has her on continual watch now in the ICU after having MRIs, X-rays, and a series of other tests. She has returned to a vegetable state since arriving at Pleasant View Hospital with her vitals dangerously low.

Nurses are administering IV medications through her port while stitching and bandaging lacerations. Her left leg is placed in a cast after being broken in the fall. It takes one nurse to look at the monitor to see her crashing. Calling for a crash cart, they give her a shot of adrenaline in hopes of raising her vitals. The doctor on the ward enters as the crash cart is rolled in. Clearing the area around her, the doctor has the pedals prepped. Applying them to her chest, he releases the current. Her body rises from the bed several inches before falling back to the padded surface. They check the monitors once more to see the red flatline steadily continuing. After several more attempts, the doctor pronounces her dead at three-fifteen in the morning. As her body is covered in the white sheet, the orderlies miss her lips curl into an insidious smirk.

"Transport her to the morgue in the service elevator." Doctor Schit instructs as he uses his index finger and thumb to rub his exhausted eyes. He is a man of short stature, short but stout with broad muscular shoulders. Under his white gowns are a blue dress shirt and black trousers. His Thinning white hair and goatee hint at his elevated age. "I want the paperwork processed before she is cold on the table. Take precautions to dot the T's and cross the I's." He remarks sarcastically before leaving the room. The orderlies look to one another but begin preparing her for transport.

    Doctor Schit enters the hall with a hand wiping his forehead. Slamming the patient folders onto the nurse's station, which is only a head shorter than he is, he rushes down the hall to the break room. Seeing it empty, he closes the door behind him before crossing the tiled floor to the counter. He pours himself a cup of coffee, leaving only two inches before filling the cup. Looking back at the door, he pulls a flask from his back pocket and pours the contents into the cup before replacing it. The smell of strong whiskey wafts from the cup before it disappears into the thick black coffee. It is several minutes before he hears the wails of fear and terror coming from the waiting room accompanying the ping of the elevator door opening.

# 5.

The lights in the halls of the hospital go out. The orderlies and staff look around for several moments waiting for the backup generators to kick in. When they don't panic, they begin to rise within the halls. Vital machines that rely on electrical energy go lifeless. Those relying on those machines gasp and panic were able to drift quietly from life. The orderlies rush to nearby rooms to perform CPR in a fruitless effort to preserve the life of patients on life support. Blinded by the sudden darkness, they wander the hospital using flashlights from utility drawers or from their cell phones. Doctor Schit stumbles in the dark, spilling the whiskey-tainted hot coffee down the front of his shirt.

"What the Hell is going on?" Schit yells out in a high-pitched voice.

"The power went out, Doc," Schit hears the maintenance man Joe call in his deep voice. The voice comes from out within the hall following a beam of light.

"No shit, Joe," Schit remarks loudly and angrily. "But why, and why is the backup generator not kicking on?"

"No clue, Doc," Joe responds as he passes the closed breakroom door. "I am on my way down to check now. Gonna be a few though, I gotta take the stairs." A shadow of the elderly janitor moves past the door before disappearing into the darkness. Doctor Schit pulls his cell phone from his pocket and uses the bright screen to investigate the coffee stain forming on his once-clean clothing. Cursing, he thumbs around on the screen before finding the flashlight. With a sigh of relief, he raises the light to find a bloodied, form of a woman standing just in front of the door.

A slender, well-curved woman with short-cropped blonde hair and coal-black eyes lurches towards Doctor Schit with an awkward and eerie silence. She wears only a hospital gown with the strings hanging loosely. The gown slips down the right shoulder, bi-curious exposing the left chill touched and perky breast. She seems not to notice or mind as she continues to walk slowly toward the good doctor who has begun to back away.

"Are you unwell, ma'am?" Doctor Schit inquires with a quivering voice. The room quickly drops thirty degrees causing his breath to rise in a clear mist.

"I can have an orderly escort you to a room where you may be seen."

"Doctor Schit," Jamie mutters in a cold, merciless voice. "How we have looked forward to meeting you."

"We?" Doctor Schit asks curiously as he backs against the far wall.

"We have watched you for years as you practiced half-assed medicine, lining your pockets with the money of the poor in exchange for empty promises of better treatment. Your greed has made you infamous. You dying patients have made you popular in our reign." Jamie whispers in an insidious tone as she closes the difference so she stands only a few feet from him. "The Taylor case really put you on our radar."

"Steven Taylor? The man with the failing liver?" Doctor Schit asks in disbelief. "I did everything for him I could."

"You charged him thirty thousand dollars," She speaks with many voices in unison. Her breath smells of burning sulfur and brimstone. Black icker drools across her chin, her tongue following to sop it up. "Thirty-thousand dollars for a liver transplant when you knew the liver was past the window of being viable. You knew it would fail. You knew he was spending money he did not have, mortgaging his family home and taking out bank loans to pay for a procedure that was doomed just as much as he was."

"I did not have access to that information until he was already prepped for surgery." Schit protests while pointing a finger at her. "I already served my punishment. I was suspended for a month,"

"With pay and full benefits while his family was thrown from their home." Jamie counters violently yelling in multiple voices before her tone is reduced to whispers. "His wife lost their children to the system before hanging herself from Marshall Memorial Bridge." She steps towards him quickly while stretching her arm out. Before Schit can blink, the palm of her hand is nestling his chin while her fingers firmly grip the sides of his face.

Jamie leans forward and licks the left side of his face with her forked tongue. The flesh dampened by her black icker saliva steams and melts away to expose muscle tissue before melting through to leave a gaping hole exposing the inside of his mouth. Schit screams, writhing in pain while firmly within her grip.

"Let me go, bitch!" Doctor Schit yells while kicking at her bare legs. His shoes kick away rotting flesh, breaking the bone running through her shin. With his lower face in her grasp, she slides him up the wall lifting his feet from the tiled floor of the breakroom. Her pink polished nail digs into his cheeks, tearing away flesh from his face as she pushes his head more firmly against the wall.

"You will like hell." She hisses while looking him in the eyes. "Eternal torment, ravaging fire, the heat will boil your blood internally. There are patients of yours, late patients, who are dying to see you again. I can not wait to tell them the doctor is in." Jamie hisses in better than six voices simultaneously. Leaning in, the elbow connected to the hand holding Doctor Schit bends at a sharp angle rearing back behind her shoulder. She growls viciously with bared teeth.

"Tell them I sent you." She snarls maliciously. With inhuman force, she pushes his head into the brick wall, crushing his skull into shards. Blood and brain matter explodes on the wall, and his eyes pop from the front of his skull, flying over her shoulder to the break room floor. They roll curiously before rolling under a table. With her fingers covered in sludgy remains of his destroyed brain matter and dust or small fragments of bone, she pulls her hand away from his crumpled head. His remains fall to the floor at her feet. Without a word, Jamie turns from the doctor and leaves the room back into the darkness of the hall. Her slender back and round cheeks reflect the light of the moon.

"Use battery-operated lights to treat the patients." A charge nurse orders from the hall as she directs her nurses. "There are hand pumps for administering oxygen. Chest compressions for the heart patients, do not overdo it though." She instructs while holding a flashlight of her own in her right hand. Claire is an overly large woman in her mid to late forties with coal-black hair and deep dimples. Standing just over six-foot, her size has proved more than intimidating over the span of her life. "Has anyone seen Joe or Doctor Schit?"

"The doctor was heading towards the breakroom," An orderly replies as he moves past her. He is in his late teens and fresh from nursing school. Kody has unkempt brown hair and blue eyes with an athletic figure from his years as a fullback in high school and college. "I haven't seen Joe, though." Kody is about to enter a patient's area when Claire stops him.

"I want you to go find him," Claire instructs sternly. "Hurry up and have him check the generators. We need lights back on here, and for the equipment to work. Otherwise, we are going to lose a lot more patients tonight." She whispers calmly. She and Kody watch as one after another, gurneys with patients covered by white sheets are wheeled away to an administrative office for storage until the lift begins to work again.

"Yes, ma'am," Kody replies with a grimace. His gaze moves away from the bodies being carted away. "Right away." Nodding to himself, Kody leaves her side to head towards the stairwell in the east wing.

Kody opens the metal door to enter the stairwell. Shining his flashlight up and down the stairs, he determines he is alone in the stairwell. That, and he does not hear any movement on the grated steps. Giving out a high-pitched whistle, he listens for several seconds until the sound dies away and the stairs are once more silent as they are dark. He steps out onto the platform, allowing the door to swing closed behind him, taking in a deep breath before beginning his descent.

"It is okay, Kody," He assures himself as he carefully makes his way to the next landing. "It is only a dark, quiet stairwell. Nothing to worry about." He shines his flashlight around the stone shaft that houses the stairs with the only form of internal support coming in the means of stone platforms two to every floor between steel grate steps. "Imagine being afraid of the dark in a hospital when the lights go out and the generator fails." Kody muses while slowly making his way to the next platform.

"Hey, Joe," He calls loudly in the vast empty space below him. "Are you down there, man?" He inquires with beads of sweat running down the back of his neck despite the chilly atmosphere of the stairwell. He waits for several minutes, listening for some sort of reply when a clatter comes from overhead. Kody looks up in time to hear the clatter continue.

"Joe, are you up there?" Kody calls in desperation. "This ain't funny, man." Repeated footsteps reverberate stairs overhead in the moments that follow his calls.

"Yo, Joe," Kody calls again while waving his flashlight overhead. "Claire Bailey wants you to check the generators." He calls with one hand cupping the side of his mouth, He listens for a few moments, hoping Joe would respond. He hopes it is Joe overhead and that Joe will acknowledge him. What he gets is something else.

"Help," A woman's voice calls down from the darkness. "Please, if you can hear me, will you help?"

"What is the matter?" Kody replies back.

"I am injured," The woman replies in a tone of panic. "They left me here on the stairs when the power went off and said they would be right back." Kody listens for a moment for any other sounds but the stairwell has gone silent waiting for a reply. Looking back at the door he had previously exited, the reflective number sixteen shimmers when the light hits it. Why would they leave her, and why does she not just go to another floor?

"Why are you stuck?" Kody inquires curiously as he shines the light up and down the stairwell once more searching for anyone else that may be on the stairs.

"I don't have a light and I am afraid of heights." The woman replies quickly. Kody shrugs and nods in understanding. He has a light and is still afraid of the dark. Enough so that he is hesitating to help a patient who is stuck on an upper floor.

"I am on my way up." Kody remarks as he begrudgingly begins to ascend the stairs. "Do you know what floor you are on?"

"Between nineteen and twenty." The woman replies with a sense of relief.

"Alright," Kody calls with his gaze fixated on the next step ahead along with the beam from his flashlight. "I am on my way. Just, just keep talking to me until I get to you so I can judge your trauma level and ease nerves." He instructs with forced casualness. He takes each step one at a time, his left hand holding the flashlight firmly while the right has a death grip on the railing.

"My name is Jamie," She introduces herself.

"I am Kody, Kody Miller." He replies with a smile. Despite his rising fear, he finds himself wondering what she looks like. She does not sound much older than him, if any, and has a sweet innocent voice. "I am an RN in the trauma unit, fresh from med school. How about you?" Kody remarks with a sense of tension as his gaze moves to the dark void beneath him. He squints his eyes closed for a moment before pushing on.

"Are you coming?" The reply comes. Kody hesitates before taking the next step. His palms are becoming clammy and his knees are beginning to quiver. An odd sensation of rolling barrels fills his abdomen and for a moment he fears they will expel from his watery mouth.

"I am on my way," Kody assures her again while moving slowly up the steps.

# 6.

Kody carefully ascends the steel grated steps with his hand firmly on the steel pipe hand railing. He continues to talk to the frantic Jamie, whom he continues to try and learn about but can only manage to get short, vague responses. Moving slowly, it takes him the better part of an hour to traverse the three floors that separate him from the troubled woman. Reaching the nineteenth floor, he looks around with sweat running down his forehead and neck. He looks around the empty landing with frustration and curiosity.

"Jamie," Kody calls out feeling short of breath. "Where are you?"

"On the landing between nineteen and twenty." The sweet innocent voice responds with terror slowly starting to fade as he shines the flashlight up the stairs. "I can see your light. Will you come to help me?"

"Is there any way you can walk down to me?" Kody inquires hopefully.

"I have fallen and hurt my ankles," Jamie replies with a wincing tone. "I can't move." Wiping his forehead, Kody shines his light up and down the stairs once more before taking back his firm grip on the steel pipe railing, it cold to his touch, and begins easing his way up one more landing.

    Kody manages to reach the next landing, hunched over while shivering from the cold and fear of the dark that is nearly paralyzing him the longer he is reduced to a small light. As he reaches the landing, the light he holds begins to flicker in rapid intervals. Kody curses desperately as he taps the flashlight on his right knee. In the fluttering light, Kody catches glimpses of something moving from one side of the landing to another. The image is fleeting and ominous. He sees trails of white cloth and pale flesh. A brief glimpse of blonde hair and nudity releasing fabric to linger on the stone floor. With each break of light is an extended period of darkness in which all Kody can see are two sinister orbs of glossy red. Kody frantically shakes the flashlight up and down while praying for it to work. With both hands on the flashlight, it aimed upward at his face, the light returned solidly. Kody is blinded briefly as the light shines directly into his eyes. Squinting firmly, he lowers the light from his eyes while rubbing them quickly. Once the burning has stopped, he looks again, shining the light around. He sees nothing but an empty landing.

"Jamie?" Kody asks with a rattling breath. "I'm here. Where are you?"

There is a brief moment of silence, of stillness in which the only thing moving is his light as he scans the landing from the left to the right. As he begins to fan it back to the left, a figure pops up in the beam of light. The figure is an intense pale that nearly reflects the light in various directions. The eyes are as red as fire, the mouth gaping open a good six inches with the corners ripped allowing for it to open broader. The teeth are broken, jagged, and charred black. The tongue rolls out in a foot-long forked tendril that lashes out at him from a black abyss. Sinister claw-like hands reach for him with ominous intent. The gloomy, pale form of a nude woman swiftly lunges at him with a blood-curdling wail.

In a frightening attempt to flee, Kody begins to turn and run. His foot slips on the edge of the stone slab, his hands coming free of the steel pipe railing. In mid-turn, Kody lunges forward falling face-first down the steel steps. He tumbles for what seems mere seconds, the flashlight coming free from his hand as he tries to catch hold of anything that will stop his rapid and painful descent. His hands are met in odd angles with grated steel, smooth, cold, and unyielding. When he comes to rest finally at the next platform, he is bent double with his face against the grit of the stone slab, his rump in the air while he rests on one bloodied knee while the other leg sticks out awkwardly to the side. A femur bone sticks from the flesh of his right leg, his right foot pointing in the wrong position.

Kody stretches out slowly on the platform with his eyes closed tightly. He fans his arms out as broken wings, his joints popping audibly as bones broken from their rightful place grind against fragments. Kody feels warm fluids spreading around him in various areas. He moans in pain, content not to move for several minutes, his mind trying to wrap around the image he had seen on the previous platform. With each movement, he cries out again and again in agonizing pain.

"Help me," Kody yells out loud, warm copper-tasting fluids creaking from the corners of his mouth. "Someone, anyone, will you please help me?" Kody yells out once more. With trembling fingers, he grips the stone platform and tries to drag himself into the darkness. The stairwell has gone eerily silent. All he can hear is his own raspy breathing.

    Kody stops, staying still on the pavement. He tries to calm his erratic breathing long enough to listen for any movement aside from his own. Lingering for several minutes, he listens intently. He moves his head around, his neck popping painfully as he trains his ears in different directions to listen for any sound that he may find in the stairwell. A pair of glossy crimson eyes watch him from overhead, just out of his sight and not making a sound.

    "Help," Kody calls out once more. "I fell down the stairs. I need help, please." Kody calls out as he begins to cry. Fear has completely filled him. He senses danger in every direction of the darkness. Looking back in the direction that he thinks the stairs to the platform between nineteen and twenty lies, he repeatedly checks to see if he can hear anyone following. "There is someone, something, after me. It pushed me down the stairs. Please, I need help." Kody calls frantically into the darkness.

Kody's right-hand finds the edge of the platform. His fingers coil around the lip as he pulls himself so he can blindly peak over the edge into more darkness. Many floors down, a door creaks open in the stairwell allowing a glimpse of light to rise and meet his gaze. He can not see the door, its occupant, or what floor it is on, but the light begins to flee as the creaking of the door closing rises to his ears.

"Help!" Kody calls quickly with a gust of breath in his lungs. He hears a rattling below and the creaking of the door stops, a faint beam of light still rising from below. "I am stuck up here," Kody adds with a quivering voice. "I fell on the steps and broke my leg. I am bleeding badly and have no light." Kody stops a moment to catch his breath, hoping that whoever it is below will help. He waits in awkward silence for several minutes before a beam of light comes traveling up the platforms slowly. Desperately, Kody pulls himself to the edge of the platform so that he is within sight. The beam of light comes across his face, hurting his eyes briefly.

"Who is there?" The voice of an elderly man travels from the depths of the stairwell.

"Joe, is that you?" Kody calls, the voice familiar to him as it echoes in the stone shaft. "It's Kody. An RN from the trauma ward." He calls down with renewing hopes.

"What ya doing up there?" Joe calls back with a puzzled tone.

"I was sent to look for you," Kody replies with a laugh.

"You would never catch my lazy ass up that high, boy," Joe remarks gruffly. "Are you up there alone?"

"I don't know," Kody admits sheepishly. "I came up here to help a woman, but when I got to her I found something else. Something that scared the shit out of me."

"I have been after those rats for a while now," Joe remarks with a tone that sounds about half distracted. Kody listens and can hear him slowly and carefully ascending the stairs one metal grate at a time. "They be some big sum' bitches, I do reckon."

"This was no damn rat," Kody calls back frantically. "Please hurry. I don't like being alone up here in the dark by myself."

"Don't be so damn pushy, boy," Joe remarks sternly. "At my age, you don't move very quickly."

161

"Be careful, there is something up here." Kody remarks as he rolls to his back in hopes of finding some relief from the pain coursing through his body. He closes his eyes, thankful someone heard his cries for help even if it is only the elderly janitor and maintenance man. With hopes, he will be in the emergency room within the next hour or so. Maybe he has a radio and can call for help. Either way, Kody is thankful he is no longer alone in the dark stairwell. He opens his eyes once more to see the glowing red orbs looking down at him from a platform just overhead.

"Joe," Kody yells in fear. "It's here. It's looking at me."

"What is it, boy?" Joe asks curiously as he continues to climb the steps toward Kody.

"It is a naked woman," Kody replies with a shrill voice.

"We should all be so lucky as to have one of them looking at us." Joe remarks with a chuckle. "Can't wait to get there myself."

"Joe, please hurry," Kody calls down, ignoring the elderly man's last statement. The piercing eyes catch his gaze. He can no longer see her form, it is hidden in the void of darkness. Only the eyes are visible. They stare as if into his soul causing his insides to burn and ache. He tries to close his eyes again but finds them locked open, fixated on her gaze.

    Frozen in fear, Kody lies on the stone platform with the back of his head resting hazardously on the edge. His eyes grow wider by the second, tears gathering in the outside corners before rolling along his temples and the sides of his head. The faintest sounds of water droplets hitting steel are lost in the still darkness. His head shrinks into his shoulders as he tries to back away from the images the eyes are portraying. In his mind's eye, Kody can see an army of dark souls shrouded in a veil-like mist. Only the red shapeless eyes meet his vision with searing flames filling the landscape. Jagged, unearthly structures loom in the background, rising to pointed peaks projecting a devilishly ominous gloom. Great winged beasts appear as small bats in the distance, their shadows on the lava and brimstone ground showing terrifically terrifying images of grander beasts carrying death between their wings.

Kody gasps, exhaling steam. His veins darken, tracing throughout his body as the whites of his eyes become bloodshot. His pupils retract while his body writhes in pain and anguish. His skin tone becomes sunburnt as if he has laid out in prolonged exposure far longer than humanly possible. Suffering in silence, his mouth remains gawking, gaping open as a thin trail of black icker is released from the entity into his readied throat. He drinks readily to replenish his dehydrated body. He feels as though he is boiling internally while the icker soothes the fire with false hopes. His retracted pupils return, magnified as he inhales deeply and begins coughing harshly.

Kody's gaze breaks as the red eyes vanish into the dark. Rolling to his right side, he gasps for air and trembles violently. He can hear the sound of feet stepping on the steel grates as Joe approaches slowly. He raises his left hand to his throat, rubbing it comfortingly as he continues to cough, not seeing the ash he expels.

"I'm almost there, boy," Joe comments with a faint breath. He struggles, gasping for air. He shines his light up the steps to illuminate Kody on the next platform up. Kody appears with ramshackle hair and bloodshot eyes. Veins stick out in his neck and temples. Blood trails from his eyes and the corners of his mouth.

"Damn, boy. You look like shit warmed over." Joe remarks with a grimace. He reaches into his tool belt and retrieves a handheld radio from a side pocket. "Yo, this is Joe. Are ya there, Chetney?" Joe remarks questioningly into the handheld as he tries to contact the chief security guard. Chetney was supposed to be listening for him to call from the first-floor desk in case he found any hazards while trying to restore the power.

"Yeah, Joe. What did you find?" Chetney replies with a casual if not bored tone.

"I have a male nurse here on..." Joe moves his flashlight to the nearest door to see what floor they are on. "He is halfway between the nineteenth and twentieth floors. He has taken a bad tumble and is in great need of medical attention." Joe relays across the radio. While talking to Chetney, Joe eases himself onto one of the grate steps to rest and catch his breath. Kody rolls back again to rest with his eyes closed. Joe leans with his right arm on his left knee as he turns to look at the young man while waiting for a response.

"Joe," Chetney comes back across the radio. "I am sending some orderlies up to you, just sit with him until they get there." He instructs quickly. "A triage room is being prepared for him."

Joe raises the radio to his mouth slowly. His tired eyes caught something moving on the platform and he is currently searching for it with his light. carefully, he stands to his feet while informing Chetney they would be waiting. While placing the radio on the platform, he reaches for a fly swatter hanging from his belt.

"Another damn rat," Joe growls in a low tone. He is busy shifting his feet around on the grate when he smells ash, burnt embers, the smell of rotten eggs. Sniffing, he traces the smell upward.

Black icker lands on his forehead. His eyes grow wide as the looming figure of a nude blonde woman with crimson red eyes, cold pale blue skin, and a gaping maw falls down head first towards him. Joe lets out a curdling scream while trying to take a step back. His left foot finds the small pool of tears resting on the narrow step before slipping out from underneath him. Joe reaches for the railing in desperation, catching himself. His feet slip and jump three steps down, bouncing on each one, but he manages to keep himself from falling bodily down the steps. Looking up again, he shines the flashlight that he managed to keep a hold of and sighs in relief when he does not see the woman again.

"Damn, Joe. you old fool. That boy done got you seeing naked demon women in the stairs." Joe scolds himself and chuckles. He wipes his forehead and turns to look down the steps only to find the woman looking at him from the steps.

She stands with her head tilted down, her stone-cold gaze looking him in the eyes. Her blond hair is tangled, resting in knots. She stands with her boney shoulders slumped, her arms dangling to her sides, her hands by her wide hips, and hunched over so her breasts tilt towards him seductively. Joe looks at her with an entranced mental condition. Her crimson red eyes are reflective in his dilated pupils. Her red pouting lips curl at the torn corners into a hideous, insidious smile as she reaches up with the index finger of her right hand to poke him in the chest.

"Jump." She instructs simply in a raspy tone, neither male nor female but numerous in voices. Joe does not remove his gaze from hers but nods in understanding.

# 7.

Joe drops his flashlight and tools onto the stairwell landing with a blank expression. He climbs gingerly onto the railing with ease and strength he has not known for years. Balancing on the railing, he teeters back and forth while overlooking the expanse of the stone shaft. The stairs wind around the outer edge of the stairwell with an empty void traversing the center. Joe's eyes roll to the back of his head with her jaw gawking awkwardly to the left. He takes one gentle step forward and vanishes within the darkness. Several fleeting moments of silence followed before the sound of crushing, crumbling bone accompanied by the splitting and splattering of warm fluids. An immediate stench of bile begins lofting up the chamber. A stench of bile, iron, and sulfur fills the air with repulsion.

    A mechanical grinding sound begins filling the chamber as a soft neon orange light begins to swirl. The air is filled with Chemical haze from the ventilation shafts. The woman turns her head sharply to the third floor with a menacing smirk.

The young attendant makes his way wearily through the chemical labs, turning on all of the gas nozzles from the bunsen burners. He has already switched on the gas flow to the hospital manually, freeing all of the major gas valves to fill the hospital with colorless and scentless gas. After locking down the hospital, the next logical course was to demolish it. Demolish it with everyone still in so the evil can not get free. A chill fills the air as he turns on the last of the burners. Pulling his lab coat closer around him, he turns towards the entrance to the lab to see the slim, petite, and withering form of a once beautiful blonde woman standing nude in the door frame.

"I suspect it's you I can thank for my hospital being overrun with evil?" He holds his left arm as it hangs loosely to his side.

"Your efforts are meaningless." She hisses in multiple voices. "Your frailty will be short-lived as we cross the threshold into your realm."

"Who are we?" He asks while slumping against a wall.

"The denizens of Hell in all of our glory." The voices singsong around him in unison. With a peal of deep insidious laughter, she takes one step and appears next to him with her hand around his throat. Extending her torso upward, she lifts him from his feet. He kicks out several times, trying to knock himself free, but her grip continues to hold him. With a final, desperate attempt to get free, he stomps down with his heel aimed directly at her nose. Her grip falters just long enough for him to pry her hand open and fall to his freedom. His legs collapse on landing causing him to land on his left side. He does not waste time scurrying to his feet and rushing across the room. He looks back only briefly to see her face ripped open to reveal a streak of a blood-stained skull on the right-hand side of her face. The flesh and hair peeled back over the temple.

"You pathetic vermin!" She calls in her many voices. "Your name is written within the pages of the Damned. I know your name, your every sin, your every weakness." She bellows after him as he rushes for the door. He stops for a moment with a quirky smile as he pushes the door open to the hall.

"Then you know to just call me Joe," He retorts with a hesitant, but strong voice. Shoving the door open, he rushes into the hall and towards the stairwell. The hospital is slowly filling with gas and despite his heroism, his plan is for self-preservation. He can make his way to the roof and have a good chance of surviving the blast. He enters the stairwell at a full sprint until the scent hits him. He collapses against the inside wall of the stairwell and covers his nose with the breast of his lab coat. He looks around and glances over the railing to the floors below. The bottommost landing to the basement is coated in a thick crimson substance. Intestine, meat, flesh, and clothing litter the steps and railing for several floors. Tufts of hair cling to the walls with grizzly trails of blood running like paint in erratic patterns.

"This is as grim a day as any man has recognized." He mutters to himself with the lower half of his face covered. He struggles to his feet, his feet slipping on the bodily fluids covering the platform where he crouches. Voices of agony begin filling the stone chamber. Heat rises from the ground causing the bile and gore to bubble and boil as the steam begins to rise in heavy vapors. Wails of anguish accompany dancing lights from hellish flames on the walls.

The rot-iron railings are replaced with skeletal bones draped with fragments of once-recognizable clothing. The iron-grated platforms begin to melt and bow under their own immense weight. Skipping every other step, Joe rushes with fleeting feet further up the stairwell before the swirling dark masses of flailing bat-like creatures appear overhead.

Joe wipes the sweat from his brow and disrobes his gown and loosens the buttons on his polo shirt. He clings to the walls of the boiling-hot stone tower. The wails push Joe to the brink of insanity. He crouches briefly, holding his hands over his ears. The anguish, sorrow, pain, hatred, and loss can not be dampened in the slightest. Tears begin to stream down his cheeks, his skin has already begun to fester under the heat creating boils and sores across his exposed flesh. He looks around helplessly for some means of escaping this chamber of torment only to find the door to the fifth floor slightly ajar a few landings above him. Climbing weakly, he crawls on hand and foot to the fifth-floor landing. The flesh from his hands sticks to the grates and peels away with each movement. The knees of his trousers char and burn away along with the soles of his slip-resistant shoes. He reaches the slightly ajar door after several agonizing minutes of treacherous travel through the ever-increasing heat. Climbing through the opening of the doorway, he slides with a sickening sound of slime and bile being smeared across a smooth surface.

The cool tile floor is an instant soothing sensation of his burnt flesh. The coolness stings in an almost pleasant way as he curls into the fetal position. The transition from the Hellishly hot stairwell into the cool interior of the fifth floor causes his body to enter a series of stages of shock. He lies freezing on the floor with swirling orange and red lights filling the blue walls of the fifth floor. Joe lifts his head and looks around the empty floor.

There are several gurneys turned over on their side littering the hall. The windows of the rooms have blood-streaked hand prints smeared along the surface or in some places blood prints of faces. There are papers and instruments scattered along the hall with an occasional sheet of paper being lifted from a cross breeze in the ventilation. Slowly, Joe climbs to his feet, stumbling with hesitant steps while clinging to the walls. His eyes are open wide in an almost eccentric expression of wonder and fear. His feet scuffle across the floor as he moves slowly and cautiously. The fifth floor, trauma ward. He looks around to see most of the doors to patients' rooms are closed. The nurses' station is empty with the entrance to the lift roped off behind the main desk.

    Joe peaks around corners to see streaks of blood, bile, and the remnants of patients lingering on the hallway floors. IV poles and abandoned wheelchairs create a rough terrain along a couple of passages, but for the moment it seems Joe is alone on this grim floor that reeks of death and malice. Aside from the beating of his own heart, the only other sound that finds Joe's ears is the hissing of gas lines on the walls and the O2 valves that have been opened. Joe looks around frantically for another way to the roof. The opposite wing's stairwell is down the west corridor, considering it as a possible exit route he begins heading that way with both hands on the wall and his feet sliding through the objects on the floor.

    "Come on, Joe," He coaxes himself in a stammering whisper. "We gotta get out of here before the place blows its top off." He continues towards the West Wing stairwell, his weak knees and failing strength slows his pace considerably while his gaze dances around the dimly lit floor for any assailant that may come his way or try to cut off his exit. He tries to move at a quicker pace, but the transition from extreme hot to extreme cold has caused his muscles to become taught, and the ligaments are stiff. His legs are weak, bowed, and contorted at odd angles causing movement to be problematic.

  The slapping of bare feet on the cold tiled floor comes from the darkness behind him. He turns back in hopes of seeing a security guard, doctor, or even another nurse, but instead, he sees a nude blonde. Half of her face is peeled away on the right-hand side of her head, revealing a grim blood-covered skull. Her body, while athletic and in pristine shape, has taken to a deep red color. Her fingers are long and spindly with long sharp talons at the peaks. Horns protrude from her head, curling much like a goat's, and large bat-like wings fan and fold from her shoulder blades. The empty eye socket on the right side of her face glows with a menacing violet hue while the one good eye on the left is replaced with a green square pupil. A thin spined tail ending in barbs and talons waves behind her as if playfully.

"Who the hell are you supposed to be?" Joe asks with an intimidated stammer.

"Joe," The echo of no less than six voices resonates from her maul of sharp teeth. Her lush lips curl into a sinister smile as she steps ever closer. Joe continues to try and put distance between her and himself, but the allure of the woman slows him even further. "I am the woman you have sought your entire life for, but always seems to slip through your grasp."

"I don't think we are compatible under the current astrological signs," Joe remarks skeptically. His faint voice betrays him as he tries to inch further away from her. "I think we should see other people before jumping into a serious relationship. Do so during a time of disaster or situations like this create weak relationships that never last." Joe rambles as he nears the entrance to the west wing stairwell.

"Joe, Joe, Joe," The nude blonde advances several more places[1] to bring her body right up against his. She smells heavily of sulfur and ash. The heat that emanates from her is reminiscent of the east wing stairwell. "You and I could raise Hell together." She sighs in several menacing voices. "I know you like what you see, even if you are afraid to admit it." She raises her arms and spins to show off her full form. She stops to face him again, her toothy smile causes a lump to form in his throat. Anxiousness and an urgency to retreat fill his senses with a tingling sensation.

"I prefer more submissive women," Joe remarks with a shrug. He moves to the door and pushes it open. "I like women who will bend to my will and do what I tell them. I'm sorry, but you seem more of the dominant type. More suited to enacting your free will." Joe exits the fifth floor into the east stairwell astonished to find he has entered a melting steel platform. The heat of the stone shaft instantly melts away the hair on his arms, chest, and legs while causing the dirty blonde hair waving on his head to curl and begin to melt slowly. His shoes begin to melt into the steel grate, sticking to the grating

---

1

pattern before he attempts to climb to the next floor. He refrains from touching the bone handrails or the bleeding, blood-boiling walls as he ascends the steps. Watching behind him, he watches as the blonde slowly follows him. She is in no hurry to keep up with his fleeing escape, she does not seem particularly concerned with him getting away.

Joe struggles to climb the remaining two floors to the roof. He exits through a pair of double doors that open out onto the helicopter platform where three paramedics lie facedown on the stone room with several small imps feasting on their corpses. Joe stops for a moment at the sight of the grizzly meal. He closes the stairwell door and bars it from outside with a crowbar lying near a toolbox close by. He can hear sneering and insidious laughter coming from within the stairwell.

"You can not escape me, Joe," Her voices echo through the door, and the vibration of the numerous voices causes the door to shiver in place. Joe looks over to the exhaust vent where the climate control unit is filtering the air in and out of the hospital. He reaches into his pocket and pulls out a Bic lighter and a scrap of paper. He looks up to see the imps looking at him with menacing gazes. The flesh of the paramedics hangs bleeding from their gnarled mouths. Sighing deeply, Joe lights the receipt paper and tosses it into the vent.

    A burst of flames erupts from the vent cover as it flows swiftly through the hospital. The imps lung at him, their talons and claws digging into his flesh, tearing him apart. Joe screams in pain while trying to run away. He crashes his body into the stone chambers of the stairwell, pinning them in turn between his body and the stone wall. They continue to tear flesh from his body with teeth and claws. Joe looks to the edge of the roof and begins running towards the four-foot wall that lines the ledge. With a final step, he leaps over the edge. He lands on the roof of the emergency room entrance sixty feet below with a sickening sound of crushing bones and splattering blood.

    The imps flutter as he descends, their wings carrying them past windows as they burst, shattering outwards as the hospital is filled with flames. One floor at a time, in rapid recession, the floors burst into flames with glass showering out over the parking lot. Distant wails of agony and despair fill the night air. Portions of various bodies, chunks of flesh, and scarred body parts land in the nearby shrubs as neighboring buildings quiver in the wake of the explosion. Three blocks on any one side of the hospital are instantly devastated. The building crumbles with shattering windows. Those made of lesser materials quickly catch flames and begin to burn. The continuous pleas for help, sympathy, or mercy go unanswered as they spread across the growing winds.

    Several streets away, the firetrucks emerge from their station with swirling red lights. Police and other first responders rush through the night traffic in the direction of the hospital. In all of the confusion of the early hour, no one notices the sinister red eyes in the early morning light. The first responders manage to salvage one patient on arrival. A young blonde woman with her head wrapped in bandages lies in nothing but a hospital gown in the bushes as the first firefighter arrives at her side. He motions for the paramedics to come to her aid and helps transfer her onto the backboard. Her skin is red from the heat of the fire and the paramedic's figure is on some broken bones. There are several lacerations where she had gone through a window.

"Ma'am, what is your name?" A young red-headed firefighter inquires while holding an oxygen mask over her mouth and nose. The woman looks at her with her one revealed eye. It is red with a dilated pupil and swollen. She shakes her head after several minutes and rolls her head to the side to fall asleep.

"You have a Jane Doe on your hands, Lee." The firefighter announces as they place her on a gurney. They are about to load her into the ambulance when the hospital fully explodes into rubble. "She is the sole survivor of this disaster too."

Made in United States
Orlando, FL
07 September 2023